FAERIE SWAP

ANTHEA SHARP

FIDDLEHEAD PRESS

FAERIE SWAP
Book 3.5 in the Feyland Series

ISBN: 9781680130270

NOTE TO READERS:
Most of this book takes place during the events depicted in *The Twilight Kingdom* (Book 3 of the Feyland Series). The storylines of *How to Babysit a Changeling* and *The Bug in the Dark Court* are woven throughout *The Twilight Kingdom*, and this book reveals the ending. *If you have not yet finished reading the first three books, be aware there are spoilers ahead!*

Recommended series reading order:
THE FIRST ADVENTURE - Book 0 (prequel)
THE DARK REALM – Book 1
THE BRIGHT COURT – Book 2
THE TWILIGHT KINGDOM – Book 3
FAERIE SWAP - Book 3.5
TRINKET (short story)
SPARK - Book 4
BREAS'S TALE - Book 4.5
ROYAL - Book 5
MARNY - Book 6
CHRONICLE WORLDS: FEYLAND
FEYLAND TALES VOLUME 1

CONTENTS

This collection is for Jack & Maggie
Keep adventuring, always~

HOW TO BABYSIT A CHANGELING

THE CAFETERIA at Crestview High was filled with the din of conversation, the clank of silverware on plasmetal trays, and somebody's tunes cranked up too loud, screeching tinnily out of their earbuds. Despite the noise, despite the smell of floor cleaner mixed with cooked cabbage, despite the fact that high school was all kinds of tedious, Marny Fanalua never let things get to her. It wasn't worth getting tangled up in small annoyances—and almost everything was small, when you took a breath and looked at it.

She sat across from her friends, slightly scruffy Tam Linn and rich-girl Jennet Carter. They'd all found out recently that life was a lot more interesting than they'd ever imagined.

A little *too* interesting at times, maybe. It wasn't every day a person discovered that their favorite sim video game was actually a portal into a treacherous magical world.

Marny leaned forward and rested her broad arms on the table, studying Tam's face. She'd known him a long time, and she could tell by the tightness around his eyes—what she could see of them behind the screen of his overlong brown hair—that something was severely wrong.

Wrong beyond the usual tweaked state of Tam's life, which was bad enough. Nobody could call scraping by in the Exe fun.

Maybe his mom had taken off again. In Marny's opinion the woman barely qualified for the title, other than the fact that she'd given birth to Tam and his little brother. So, either his mom had gone off her meds and left Tam and the Bug in the lurch again, or something freaky was going on.

And if it was something freaky, that meant magic. Fey magic.

"Okay, spill it," she said.

Jennet sent her a grateful half-smile, but Marny stayed focused on Tam. He clenched one hand, then smoothed it out flat over the scraped tabletop. Before speaking, he shot a quick glance at the neighboring tables, but nobody was paying attention to them. Why should they? She and Tam were misfits—always had been. And Jennet had become a lost cause to the status-conscious Viewer kids since becoming Tam's sort-of girlfriend.

"They've taken my little brother," Tam said, his voice tight.

Oh, crap. Marny narrowed her eyes. Tam's brother, the Bug, was a sweet kid, if a bit random.

"*They*, as in the Dark Court faeries?" she asked. Tam nodded, and coldness settled in the pit of her stomach. "How do you know?"

"I know because they left a changeling creature in his place." Tam swiped his hair out of his eyes. "My brother is being held hostage in the Realm of Faerie by the Dark

Queen, in payback for Jennet and me meddling between the realms."

"Yeah well, your *meddling* is kind of crucial." Marny folded her arms. "It's keeping the fey from stealing human energy and opening a gateway to the mortal world. Stopping blood sacrifice. Little things like that."

"We never thought they could do something like this, though," Jennet said. "Tam's brother is in serious danger."

She would know, too, having encountered the queen a few times too many. The back of Marny's neck prickled. Personally, she was glad to have never encountered that particular being. One of the advantages of staying out of sim games. Especially Feyland, which had managed to use the game interface to open a gateway from the Realm of Faerie to the mortal world, with serious consequences.

"Also, my mom's gone again," Tam said, his gaze dropping to the dingy floor, as if it were his fault the woman had problems.

Double serving of trouble for Tam, then. Marny shook her head.

"How do we get your little brother out of Feyland?" she asked.

"We're working on that from the inside," Jennet said, laying one pale, slim hand on Tam's shoulder. "We'll get him back."

"Meanwhile there's a creature living in my house." Tam shoved his tray away, food uneaten. "I can't leave it there alone all the time."

Marny took a deep breath, instantly regretting it as the smell of overcooked spaghetti filled her nose.

"So, just to be clear—the Bug's been stolen away by the

faeries, and they left a substitute in his place?" she asked. "One that's now living with you?"

Tam nodded miserably.

"I want to meet him. It. Whatever," Marny said, before she even knew the words were going to come out of her mouth. Yet, it made perfect sense for her to get involved.

"What?" Tam jerked his head up, denial flashing through his green eyes.

"Look." She spread her hands wide. "You two have to deal with things in-game. The last thing you need to worry about is some freaky faerie dude pretending to be the Bug. Even though I don't sim, I can help with this."

Jennet nodded and looked at Tam. "She's right. We can't take care of the changeling, and beta testing Feyland, and everything else that's going on—not by ourselves."

"At least your mom's not around," Marny said. "It's crappy that she's gone, but the timing is decent. Considering. This way, if she comes home and you guys are, um, unavailable, I can run interference."

Tam and Jennet needed to get back in-game to try and rescue the Bug. And Marny *had* encountered the magic and creatures of Feyland before. She was up for this.

Looking after the changeling thing couldn't be much worse than the few times she'd babysat Tam's actual little brother, right? That kid was a ball of crazy energy.

The hubbub in the cafeteria was dying down, the tables emptying out.

"Okay." Tam swiped a hand through his hair. He looked like he'd barely gotten any sleep. "Marny, if you're free you can come over after school today and meet the changeling. Provided it's still there."

"It will be," Jennet said. "I think changelings have to stay close to home. Their pretend home, I mean. I'll read up in my folklore book and let you know what else I find out."

"Good." Marny nodded, her black hair tickling her cheek. "This should be interesting."

Tam and Jennet could have their adventures inside Feyland.

Gaming was fine, and she was good at it, as long as she wasn't simming. But Marny had always felt that real life contained more than enough weirdness for a person to deal with. And she never had figured herself for hero material, anyway. Sure, she was competent and smart and strong, but there were better-qualified people when it came to saving the world.

It wasn't Marny's idea of a fun time, going on foot through the Exe—basically the ghetto of Crestview—but there was no other way to get to Tam's house. They'd met up after school and she followed him down stinking alleys, stepping over puddles slimed with oil and decay. Past graffiti-layered build- ings with broken windows staring like blind eyes, and through gang territory where a misstep could bring trouble raining down on their heads.

She was large, both taller and wider than Tam, and could handle herself in a fight—though probably not against an entire Exe gang. Still, she had a knife strapped to her calf, and the can of pepper spray her uncle insisted she carry every- where. She and Tam would be all right.

But it wouldn't come to that. So far, they hadn't met any

trouble. Even though she was big, she knew how to move silently as they picked their way deeper into the Exe.

Without speaking, Tam led her down the last block before his house. They carefully skirted the broken building where the yellow-eyed smoke drifters squatted. Marny wrinkled her nose against the sickly sweet smell, glad to see Tam's place up ahead.

The house was a rickety, two-room building perched on the flat roof of an old auto-repair shop, long closed. A blue tarp gone tattered and gray flapped across part of the shelter's roof, and the walls were patched with scabby pieces of corrugated metal.

Marny followed Tam up the rickety staircase on the side of the building. The railing wobbled under her hand.

"Watch the seventh tread," Tam said. "It's pretty rotted."

Yeah, last thing he needed was for a big Samoan girl to crash through and ruin his stairs. She skipped the seventh one, then waited at the top of the landing behind Tam as he used his ring of jingling keys to open the multiple deadbolts. Old tech, but reliable. It was too easy to hack a keypad system, and the authorities didn't care if your stuff got stolen, not here in the Exe. She doubted the cops even came out this far.

Tam slipped his keys into his back pocket. A shadow moved behind the wire-webbed window next to the door. Tam held up his hand, signaling her to wait, then pushed the door open and slipped inside.

Everything was quiet for a heartbeat. Two. Marny peered through the half-open door.

"Hiiiyyaaa!" a voice screeched.

The sound was wrong, something made from an

inhuman throat. The hairs on Marny's arms rose. She banged open the door, to see a small creature clinging to Tam's shoulders. Its clawed hands were tangled in his hair, and bright eyes gleamed maliciously from a pale, wizened face.

"Hey!" Tam yelled. "Get off."

He tried to shake the thing loose, but it held on tight, like some gruesome parody of a kid taking a pony ride on its dad's shoulders.

"Gotcha!" The creature laughed, showing sharp teeth.

Marny was through the door in two steps. She swept up her right arm and put some power behind it. Not quite a punch, but enough to send the oddly-jointed creature tumbling down. It flew off Tam's shoulders, its screeching laughter ending in a squawk as it landed on the carpet.

"Nice," she said, staring at the creature's bulbous, eerie-looking eyes. Its skin had a greenish tinge.

"What is this?" it hissed, glaring up at them. "Another human to see me? Sheer folly."

Tam pivoted and shut the door, snicking the locks home. "What was that about, jumping on me?"

She could see Tam's urge to kick the changeling in his face—but he'd warned her and Jennet that however the changeling was treated, the same thing would happen to the Bug. Which meant no beating up the evil faerie creature, no matter how totally deserved.

"Tee-hee. 'Twas all a bit of fun. Surprised you, did I?" The changeling grinned up at Tam and leaped to its feet. "Now feed me."

"Quite a houseguest you have there," Marny said. Maybe she shouldn't have volunteered for changeling-sitting duty after all. "As annoying as your little brother is, I prefer the Bug to *this*."

"What you think matters little to me," the changeling said.

Marny rolled her eyes at Tam and followed him into the kitchen. He flipped the electric kettle on to boil, then rummaged around in the cupboards. There didn't seem to be much to eat. Dried noodle packets, a couple lonely cans of synth-meat. Tam grabbed a few protein bars and banged the cupboard doors shut.

"Here," he said, flipping a bar through the air to the changeling.

The creature caught it and held it up to the light. "What is this item?"

"Food," Tam said, then gave Marny an exasperated look as the changeling bit into the protein bar right through the plastic packaging.

"Feh." The creature spit on the floor. "Mortal sustenance used to taste much better."

"You don't eat the wrapper," Marny said. "Peel it, like this."

She took a bar from Tam and tore off the shiny plastic. The changeling watched her, then stripped off the wrapper and popped the whole bar into his mouth.

"Still tasteless," he said, squinching his already-wrinkled face into a sour expression.

"At least we agree on that," Marny said, handing her bar to Tam.

"What?" he said. "You don't like synthesized nut-flavored protein bars?"

"I prefer my uncle Zeg's cookies."

And it was obvious Tam didn't have a lot of food in his cupboards. She wasn't hungry, and even if she were, she wouldn't eat up his few supplies.

"Me too," he said, "but I don't have any of those lying around. Tea?"

"Yeah—mint if you've got it." Tea was cheap, and it would be rude to completely refuse his hospitality.

Tam pulled out two mugs and a packet of tea bags. Marny noticed he scarfed down two of the protein bars. Right—he hadn't had any lunch. Not that school lunch was any better than the dry, non-flavored bars.

"So." She turned to the changeling, squatting on the floor like a toad. "What's your name?"

"Are you trying to trick me, mortal?" His gleaming eyes narrowed.

She raised an eyebrow. "As in...?"

"Names have power in the Realm," Tam said. "Generally, they aren't freely given out."

Marny pursed her lips. Made sense. She took the cup of tea Tam handed her.

"Right," she said. "Then what shall we call him?"

Tam frowned and shot a look at the creature. "I've been thinking of him as not-Bug."

"Catchy—but we can do better." She looked down at the fey creature again. "Changeling, what name do you use when you're in the mortal world? Doing, you know, baby imper-sonations."

The changeling folded its spindly arms and glared up at her. "I am called by the child's name."

"Yeah." Tam set his mug of tea on the counter. "Except we

know you're not my little brother. Either you choose something, or we will."

"Yoda," Marny said, laughing internally at the idea of naming the creature after an ancient film character.

"Too obvious." Tam looked the changeling over. "How about... Bilbo."

"Nah." Marny was too fond of the Hobbit characters to give this ugly creature one of their names. "If anything, it's a Gollum."

She was glad Tam still remembered the moldering old paper book they had both read the summer they were ten. Had the author based his stories on glimpses of the Realm?

"Stop." The changeling bared his pointed teeth. "If you insist, you may call me Korrigan."

He made a mighty leap up onto the counter and took a guzzling sip of Tam's tea.

"Hey, that's mine!" Tam reached for his mug, then paused, probably thinking he didn't want to put his lips where the changeling's had just been. "Fine. Drink up."

With an evil, triumphant grin, Korrigan slurped the tea down. The thing had no manners at all. When he was done, the counter was splattered with liquid. He let out a belch that sounded like a bellowing frog, and wiped his mouth with the back of his hand. Although he seemed satisfied, Marny kept a tight hold on her own mug, just in case.

"Well, mortals," he said. "I cannot set foot over the threshold of this dwelling unless Tamlin is with me."

"And thank goodness for that," Marny muttered under her breath. Crestview sure didn't need a rude changeling creature running loose through the Exe.

Korrigan shot her a narrow-eyed look, then continued.

"Since I am trapped in this wretched space, what is there to do here that will amuse me?"

"What do you normally do?" she asked.

"I squall and mewl like an infant. I flail my arms and legs, and lie in the cradle."

"Doesn't sound all that fun." In fact, it sounded stupefyingly boring.

She'd bet good credits the changeling was happy to be recognized as a faerie instead of having to pretend otherwise. Although maybe *happy* wasn't an apt word. Korrigan seemed a grumpy thing at best.

"So, you usually pretend to be much younger children," Tam said. "Why did they send you this time?"

The changeling frowned, and Marny changed her opinion from grumpy to hideously grumpy.

"It is how the thing is done," Korrigan said. "There cannot be a taking without a replacement. Most stolen children are but infants. Your brother is a special case."

That was true enough, though Marny refrained from pointing it out. Just because the Bug was all kinds of random and had tried to burn down the house a couple times didn't mean he deserved to be spirited away into the Realm of Faerie.

"Yeah," Tam said, crossing his arms. "He's a hostage."

He sounded tired and depressed, like he was about ready to give up on everything. Marny could see that losing his brother felt like the last straw.

"Tam," she said, "did you get any sleep last night?"

He shook his head in a quick, sharp negation. The shadows under his eyes were proof enough that he was exhausted.

"Go lie down," she said. "I'll show Korrigan a few basic screenie games, okay? That should keep him busy and out of trouble."

Plugging kids into screen entertainment was a time-honored tactic for keeping them occupied, and she had a feeling it would work with Korrigan. She'd guess that part of his nastiness was from sheer boredom at being marooned in the human world. Not all of his foul temper, of course. He was a fey creature from the Dark Court after all.

Yet maybe if she treated him decently, someone would do the same for the Bug.

Worry zinged through her at the thought of Tam's little brother. But they couldn't help him right now. They were doing everything they could—and for her, that meant making sure Tam got some sleep and keeping his unwelcome guest distracted and out of trouble.

"Just don't let him onto the 'net," Tam said.

"Bug's account is locked out, right?" She glanced to the corner of the living room, at Tam's netscreen setup.

She could imagine the trouble Korrigan could get into with unfettered worldwide 'net access. Not a pleasant prospect.

"Yeah," Tam said. "Log him into that, it should be fine."

He yawned, and Marny gave him a push toward the single bedroom. It was where his mom usually slept, but since she was gone...

"Get some rest," she said. "I'll introduce the changeling to the joys of Kart racing."

"Show no mercy," Tam said, heading for the bedroom.

"I won't." She grinned.

It would be fun taking the creature down a notch. And

really, even if Korrigan got super cranky, she could always just sit on him.

As soon as the bedroom door closed, Korrigan began leaping about. He bounded onto the back of the shabby couch that doubled as Tam's bed, and looked like he was going to make a leap for the light fixture.

"Chill," Marny said. "Or I won't give you any more protein bars."

"They are like eating dirt," the changeling said, but he subsided, sprawling his knobby legs out.

"You still gobbled it up quick enough." She wondered what he'd think of chocolate. Or that crazy-sweet sugar cereal the Bug liked.

On second thought, maybe hopping Korrigan up on sugar and caffeine wasn't a brilliant idea.

He made a face at her. "You see too much, mortal girl. It is not usual for a human to perceive my real form. Why, I wonder, were you able to?"

Marny went to the screen setup and flicked the power on. She could think of at least one good reason.

"I've had faerie ointment smeared around my eye," she said.

It was weeks ago, but maybe the effects were long term. Unsettling, the thought that she'd be able to see any fey folk hanging out in the human world. Not a power she was comfortable with—but it seemed like she'd have to accept it.

Korrigan shuddered. "Nasty human potion. Unfair, to see through our glamours so easily."

"Yeah, well making that potion nearly trapped my friends in the Realm forever. So I'd say it was pretty hard won."

She picked up the two gaming controllers and gave

Korrigan a hard look. It was probably a good bet he'd never driven a car in his immortal life.

"Have you ever ridden on a wild beast?" she asked.

He grimaced. "Aye, the Hunt took me up and brought me to the queen, where my servitude as a changeling began. Not a ride I would wish to repeat."

Marny nodded. She'd heard the Wild Hunt once, strange and eerie over the streets of Crestview. The clear cry of a horn had floated over the barking of eldritch hounds and the thud of hoof beats racing through the sky. She was just as glad never to have seen the elfin knights on their red-eyed mounts—and especially not the horned Master of the Hunt. It was enough hearing Tam and Jennet talk about the fearsome riders.

"Okay." She studied the changeling's wrinkled face. "You've never hopped on a fox's back and steered it with its ears or anything?"

"Not if I wanted to keep my legs," Korrigan said. "The vulpine creatures of the Realm are not to be trifled with."

"Then we'll have to take this slow." Marny handed him the controller, which he immediately brought to his mouth. "Stop! It's not something you eat."

Korrigan wrinkled his nose and examined the plastic buttons. "Then what good is it?"

"Watch."

Marny booted up the kart racing game and quickly selected the easiest mode and course. She chose her favorite vehicle, the blue one with dark green stripes.

"This is my racer," she said. "I control the speed and direction here." She demonstrated the controls, pushing the buttons and levers that made her kart move.

Korrigan looked at the netscreen, then back to the hunk of plastic in its hands. "It is a magical device?"

"I guess you could say that." She supposed the mechanics of remote-controls and screenie games were close enough to magic.

"What else might I command?" The changeling pivoted and pointed the remote at the kitchen cupboard. "Bring me a bar."

When nothing happened, he threw the controller to the floor.

"It doesn't work that way," Marny said. "You can only influence things on the screen. Which is this." She leaned forward and tapped the side of the netscreen.

"Will it produce food and drink, or fetch items from the Realm?" Korrigan asked.

"No, it just plays games. But it's fun. Now pick a kart." She pulled up the choices and used her remote as a pointer. "Do you like any of these?"

The changeling peered at the screen. "The one on the end, with the flames."

"Good pick. Now grab your controller and I'll show you how to move. Then we'll race."

Korrigan picked up the basics surprisingly quickly, and before long was zipping around the track, muttering under his breath as he tried to catch up with Marny. He screeched with glee whenever he passed one of the game-controlled racers.

"Putrid bog fungi!" he cried as his kart spun off the course yet again.

"You're taking that turn too fast," Marny said.

"My velocity matches yours," he replied, grunting as he waved the controller and got his vehicle turned back around.

"Yeah but I've got a few years of experience on you."

"But I am a fey creature, and you but a mortal girl."

"A mortal girl who's kicking your ass," she said. Still, maybe she was being too hard on him. "Do you want to try something different?"

He glanced at her, his pale eyes slitted. "Are you trying to trick me?"

"Always with the suspicion. No—I'm offering you some other options." She scrolled to a new course, featuring a race through the mushroom swamp instead of the colorful hills. "Let's do this one."

"Ah." Korrigan leaned forward, his ugly mouth splitting into a grin. "This is much more pleasant in aspect."

"All right, then." Clearly, the changeling's idea of pleasant involved copious amounts of muck and slime.

The timer counted down, and at the buzzer they took off, their bright cars zipping through the murky trees. Marny lagged a little, letting Korrigan stay close, but by the end of another hour, his skills had improved enough that she didn't need to give him a handicap. She still beat him in the overall scores, though.

"Hey." Tam opened the door of the bedroom and rubbed his eyes. "You still here, Marny?"

"Yep." She glanced out the wire-webbed window. "Getting dark."

"You're not walking home by yourself," Tam said.

"And you're not walking back alone after dropping me off," she said. "I'll ask Uncle Zeg to come get me. It's not that far." She pulled out her messager and sent her uncle a quick note.

"As if that racketing guzzler of his is low profile. I can't believe he keeps that old car running."

"We'll be okay. Zeg can out-drive anything."

"I want to race more," Korrigan said, leaping on to the back of the couch. "Next time, I will be victorious, I am certain of it."

"You can practice against the game," Tam said. "You don't need a real person to play with."

The changeling made a face, but turned back to the netscreen and soon was accelerating through the swamp once more.

"You feeling better?" Marny asked, giving him a hard look.

The smudges beneath his eyes weren't quite as dark, and his mouth seemed less pinched with exhaustion and strain.

"Adequately," he said.

"The beta team plays tomorrow afternoon, right?" she asked.

"Yes." He ran a hand through his hair, then let the strands fall back into his face. "I hope Jennet and I can get some answers. We have to figure out how to make the game safe for normal players, instead of them getting sucked into the Realm."

"I'll come over after school again," Marny said. "Keep the freaky dude out of trouble."

"Okay. I'll get you the extra set of keys for the front door." Tam glanced at the creature squatting on the couch, and misery flashed through his eyes. "I guess that's all we can do right now."

Marny patted his shoulder. "Hang in there."

She couldn't promise that everything would come out okay—who could? But she knew they'd all try.

It was a sign of how upset and distracted Tam was that he didn't ask Marny how she was getting to his house that afternoon. After school, he caught a ride to the beta testing with Jennet, giving Marny a halfhearted wave as they pulled away.

She'd planned ahead, though, and arranged for her uncle to drop her off at Tam's on his way up to the VirtuMax compound. Going alone into the Exe was plain stupid.

In fact, Uncle Zeg was the only member of her family who knew she was, as she'd put it, "helping Tam with a project at his place." Her mom would freak if she knew Marny was in the Exe without Tam, and Grandma Harmony would lecture her, then insist on telling her for the thousandth time all the ways to keep the *aitu*, or ghosts, away.

Marny went up the creaky stairs to Tam's place, undid the multiple locks on the front door, then waved to Uncle Zeg. He putted away, leaving a cloud of oily smoke in the middle of the potholed street.

It was nice to be out of the house and have some breathing room, even if she had to share that room with a fey creature. Babysitting Korrigan made a nice change from the bustling, close quarters of her own home. It wasn't that much bigger than Tam's place, and felt smaller, with her younger brother's projects always underfoot, her older twin sisters arguing night and day, Dad's boisterous jokes, and Grandma Harmony's weird teas scenting the air with bitter and pungent herbs.

Marny pushed Tam's front door open. She was greeted by a swath of vines sporting bright, poisonous-looking flowers. More plants lurked in the corners, fringed with sharp teeth.

"Jump on me, and you're meat," she called as she stepped into the jungle of Tam's living room.

From overhead, Korrigan let out an unhappy sigh. He let himself down, hand-over-hand, on one of the ropey vines hanging from the ceiling. Squatting on the floor, he blinked up at her. He almost seemed happy to have company.

"What's with the foliage?" she asked, batting away a tendril that tried to fasten around her wrist.

"This human habitation is far too plain," Korrigan said. "I thought to enliven the surroundings."

Marny kicked at a groping root. "Well, how about you un-enliven things. I'd prefer not to be some plant's snack."

"I doubt it would find you palatable," the changeling said.

Marny gave him a look, and he sniffed and waved his hands in a complex series of gestures. The vines curled up into the ceiling and the hungry-looking plants in the corner disappeared. A nearby orange flower imploded with a fleshy pop, leaving a wet spot on the dingy carpet.

"Better." Marny dug in her pack and held out a handful of silver-wrapped protein bars. "I brought you a treat."

The changeling's eyes lit, and he snatched the bars from her as if he were starving. Quickly, he stripped off the wrappers and stuffed all three bars in his mouth at once. Brown drool ran from the corner of his mouth, and Marny had to turn away from the disgusting sight. At least she'd been right that, despite his complaining, Korrigan liked the taste of the protein bars. Either that or he was really really hungry all the time.

Good thing she had another half dozen bars in her pack. Never knew when bribery would come in handy.

"Ready for some racing?" she asked.

Korrigan wiped his mouth with the back of his hand. "I shall defeat you this time."

"Yeah, we'll see about that." She was tempted to let him win once or twice, but it felt too patronizing. The changeling was quick and clever. When he came in first, beating her, it would be on his own merits.

Marny flicked on the netscreen system, and soon she and Korrigan were jockeying for position as they sped through colorful caverns. He was getting much more skilled, she'd give him that—but he still wasn't as good as she was. They played for two hours, and she let him come in a close second a few times, to keep his spirits up.

"Okay, break time." Marny tossed the controller on the couch, then stood up and stretched.

Korrigan pouted, until she gave him another protein bar.

"So," she said. "What's it like, where you're from?"

The changeling let out a heavy sigh. For a moment the sneer fell away from his mouth.

"It is full of magic and mystery. Your mortal world is nothing but drab and weary." He flicked the brown carpet with one finger.

"You've only seen the inside of Tam's house," Marny said. "There's a lot more to discover. I bet you'd be impressed with the ocean."

"We have seas in the Realm," he said with a sniff.

Still, she suspected he'd like to get out of the tiny house at some point. Maybe she and Tam could figure out a field trip. Though she really hoped the Bug would be returned soon.

"Why don't you go back there for a quick visit, and let Tam's brother come home for a bit?" she asked.

"The queen would never allow it." Korrigan shivered, then grabbed his game controller. "Let us commence racing."

Although Marny wanted to press for more information about the Dark Queen, she could tell Korrigan was done with that subject. For now.

They spent another hour mindlessly racing, until the rattle of the gas guzzler outside and the jingle of the locks signaled that Tam was home. He stepped through the door just as Marny scored another victory.

"Noo!" Korrigan flung down his controller.

"I win. Again." She glanced up at Tam. "Hey, how'd the beta testing go today?"

"Good." He sounded a little more upbeat. "I'll tell you about it tomorrow at school. Zeg's out there waiting for you."

"I know—the sound of his car is unmistakable." She rose and gathered up her back and coat. "See you later, Korr. Better work on those driving skills."

The changeling stuck his tongue out at her and crossed his eyes. "I shall master this ridiculous mortal game yet."

"He's totally hooked, poor guy." Marny shook her head, then headed for the door. "See you tomorrow."

She hoped whatever Tam and Jennet had managed to accomplish in-game, they were that much close to bringing the Bug home.

Marny was tucking her things in her backpack at the end of the school day when Jennet came rushing up, her big blue eyes wide.

"We need your help," she said.

"As in?" Marny closed up her pack, then looked at Jennet. There was a pleading in her friend's expression she mistrusted.

"Um. Tam's taking Roy Lassiter to his place to see the changeling, and you have to go with them."

"What? That's a terrible idea."

Not just having to share air with Roy, but exposing Korrigan to any more people. She was starting to feel oddly protective of the ugly little guy.

"I know." Jennet pressed her lips together in the way she did when she was upset. "But we have to prove to Roy that Tam's little brother is a hostage in the Dark Realm, so he'll let me and Tam use his sim equipment to get into Feyland. The only way to do that—"

"Is to introduce him to Korrigan. I see." Marny crossed her arms. "You better hope Roy doesn't sell you and Tam out. If your dad finds out you two are spending illicit in-game time together, things could get even more severe."

"I know. But saving the Bug is more important than whether my dad grounds me for a year. Now, will you come?"

Marny let out a sigh. Of course she'd go. She picked up her backpack.

"Fine," she said. "Lead on."

She couldn't help grimacing when she saw Royal Lassiter standing outside with Tam. Ever since Roy had used his faerie glamour on her to make her play Feyland, she'd pretty much detested him. Not only had he forced her in-game despite her claustrophobia, he'd also made her have a disgusting crush on him. The boy had a very sketchy sense of decency.

Jennet gave Tam one of her *Iloveyou* smiles. "Message me when you get up to the View, and I'll meet you at Roy's. Good luck."

Roy made a noise of disgust, either at the little love darts coming out of Tam and Jennet's eyes whenever they looked at each other, or the fact that Jennet was sure he'd let them onto his sim system. Probably both.

Marny turned her shoulder to him, and stayed a couple feet behind as he led them to the parking lot where his shiny red grav-car was parked.

"I'm sitting in back," she said as Roy waved the doors open. "Tam can enjoy the pleasure of your company."

She didn't even want to brush up against him acciden-tally. She couldn't believe she'd once actually wanted to kiss the guy. Of course, she'd been under a spell, but still. She'd rather kiss Korrigan, who at least was honest with his bad self.

Roy slid behind the wheel and started the car.

"I don't suppose you have a real address I can put in the navbot?" he asked Tam, sounding all superior.

"Not so much." Tam's voice was calm, but Marny could see him flexing his fingers. "I'll tell you how to get there."

As they drove to the Exe, Marny braced herself against Roy's wild driving and watched the neighborhoods change. Already faded and dumpy around Crestview High, they quickly disintegrated until all pretense of normal suburbia was gone. Half the buildings were empty, and the other half, Marny didn't want to know who lived inside.

"You sure it's safe?" Roy asked, slowing to navigate over a pile of rubble in the street.

"Of course it's not," Marny said. "Just do what Tam says, and we should be all right."

She was a little worried Roy would get all bossy and make his own decisions, which couldn't end well for them. Luckily, he showed some good sense, following Tam's directions as they wound through the outskirts of the Exe.

They got to an area Marny recognized. Sure enough, Tam's blue tarp roof came into view. He pointed to the alley beside the old auto shop.

"Pull up over there," he said. "And put the alarm on."

"Of course," Roy said. "It's triple-alarmed."

Not as alarmed as Roy would be if somebody decided to mess with his car. As if a siren would stop anyone.

"You seriously live here?" Roy asked, and Marny wanted to punch the smug expression off his face.

"Shut it," she said. "Welcome to the real world, rich boy."

Some day, she hoped Roy would get his comeuppance. Something that would shake his world, like being disowned by his rich CEO mom, or falling in love with a girl he could never have.

As soon as the car stopped, Tam slipped out and hurried up the stairs. Marny and Roy followed, though she hung back. The last thing she wanted was Roy behind her, where she couldn't see what he was up to.

Tam had the door open by the time they got to the top of the stairs. Inside, his living room was back to being a crazy jungle. Marny laughed a little, quietly. She hoped one of the flowers took a bite out of Roy's arm.

"Korrigan?" Tam called as they stepped into the house.

The smell of rank vegetation filled the air, and orange flowers with serrated teeth grew on ropey vines hanging from the ceiling. There seemed to be a waterfall in the kitchen, too. Nice touch.

"You have a way with decorating, Exie," Roy said. Beneath the bravado in his voice, she could hear fear.

He reached a finger out to touch one of the flowers, then jerked it back when the blossom opened its mouth and hissed at him.

Marny reached into her pack and pulled out a protein bar. Better to lure the changeling out than risk another ambush.

"Come out, Korr," she called. "I've got a treat for you."

The leafy canopy overhead rustled, and Korrigan stuck his head out.

"Protein bar? Give it to me." He stuck out his hand, his claws extended.

"A little less jungle, please." She held the bar out of reach and waggled it back and forth. "And ditch the carnivorous flowers."

He grimaced. "You mortals have no appreciation for the spice of danger."

Marny glared at him, and Tam let out a frustrated breath.

"We have more than enough danger going on right now," he said. Then he glanced at Roy, who looked way uncomfortable. "Seen enough?"

"Yeah." Roy swallowed, his gaze darting from Korrigan, to the flowers now smacking their lips, to the slick yellow moss under their feet.

"So, you believe us?" Tam pressed.

"Fine, fine. You were right." Roy looked up at the

changeling and winced. "I guess if we can be transported to Feyland, its creatures can come out."

"You have no idea," Tam said. "Let's go."

Marny nodded. Korrigan loved an audience—maybe a little too much. As soon as the boys cleared out, she'd be able to get the changeling to clean up the jungle, and then distract him with more racing.

"One sec," Roy said, pulling out his sleek messenger. "Let me vid this."

Holding it up, he slowly turned in place, panning the room. When he got to Korrigan, he paused and Marny could see him zooming in.

"Smile," she said to Korrigan.

The changeling obliged, grinning wide enough to show his pointed teeth. His eyes slitted nearly shut, and the proportions of his face were very clearly inhuman.

"Nice." Roy thumbed the power off and tucked his messenger away.

Marny wasn't too worried that Roy would try to do anything stupid with the images, like post them out on the 'net. Stuff like that could be faked all too easily, and everyone knew it, even with someone swearing eyewitness testimony.

"No more water features in the kitchen, ok?" Tam gave the changeling a stern look.

Korrigan grimaced back, but made no promises.

Marny hid her smile. Tam should know better by now not to try to bargain with the fey folk. Even she, who had only a fraction of the experience dealing with them, knew how tricksy they could be.

"You guys go have fun," she said to Tam. "I'll make him clean up. I have the rewards, you know."

"Protein bars." Tam sounded disgusted. He was probably just jealous he hadn't figured out how fond of them the changeling actually was.

"Go," she said. "And be careful."

Despite her earlier words, Tam wasn't going to sim for fun. Tam, Jennet, and Roy were headed back into Feyland. And no matter the growing fondness Marny felt for Korrigan, she really hoped they'd be able to get Tam's brother home. Soon.

"You be careful, too," Tam said. "Keep the door fully locked."

Oh, she would. The Exe might not be full of faerie peril, but there was plenty of human danger. Everything from the fact that Tam's mom could come home at any moment, which was more complication than threat, to the packs of gangs who roamed the crumbling streets, to the yellow-eyed smoke drifters who squatted in the abandoned building down the street.

As soon as Tam and Roy left, she did up all the locks, smacking the deadbolts home and sliding the chains and bars across. Then she turned to Korrigan.

"Race?" he asked, his bulbous eyes bright.

"How about you clean up, first."

He groaned, sounding like a human teenager, but the vines curled into the ceiling and disappeared, and the waterfall slowly gurgled away down the kitchen sink drain.

"Better." Marny tossed him the second remote, then settled on the couch.

"I shall beat you this time, mortal," Korrigan said.

He tried, too. For nearly two hours they raced and zoomed, and the changeling managed to push Marny to her limit. She was hanging on to her wins, but just barely.

At last, back on the mushroom swamp course, Korrigan edged past her on a turn, and cackled.

"Prepare to lose," he said, his voice high with glee.

Marny bit her lip and pushed her speed to the max, but it was too late. With a screech of triumph, the changeling crossed the finish line a moment before her.

"Heehee!" he cried. "Victory is mine."

"Good job."

He'd worked hard for that win, and it was worth it to see the goofy grin on his ugly face. Who would have thought a faerie would enjoy playing screenie games so much?

Then his expression sobered and he lifted his head, all trace of gleefulness gone. He looked dangerous now, like the fey creature from the Dark Court he truly was.

"Someone approaches," he said, his gaze moving to the wire-webbed window.

Marny hit the pause button, cutting off the happy music tinkling from the speakers. The back of her neck prickled with unease.

"Is it Tam?" she asked, already knowing the answer.

"No." The changeling screwed up his face. "Many men, with evil intent."

Crap, and double crap. Either a gang or the drifters. She'd bet credits someone had spotted Roy's fancy red grav-car parked outside earlier, and drawn the wrong conclusions about what riches might lie inside Tam's house.

Reaching past Korr, she clicked off the lamp—a clunky brass fixture with old-fashioned wiring instead of a sensor plate. The netscreen sent a pale glow over them, the word

PAUSED blinking like a silenced alarm. From the street below, Marny heard voices.

Then the clomp of footsteps on the stairs.

Crash!

She jumped at the sound of splintering wood. Somebody yelled, then cursed loudly, and she guessed they'd gone right through the rotted seventh step.

Her hand went to the knife strapped on her leg, under her jeans—but that was for closer fighting, one-on-one. It was not the right weapon to deal with a group assault.

Her heart thumping out a heavy beat in her chest, Marny slowly rose. The locks on the door would keep the intruders out. She hoped.

Korr gave her a quizzical look, and she held up her hand, signaling him to stay there.

"Hey!" The voice was accompanied by someone pounding at the door. "We know you're in there. Listen, just give us all your money, and we won't come in and hurt you."

As if Marny would crack the door open and simply hand over any nonexistent cash. Must be smoke-drifters; gang members would be more clever in their approach.

Which was good, and bad. Drifters were dumb, having numbed their brains with too much smoke. But it could also make them stupidly persistent when any normal person would go away after a while.

"I am ready to fight," Korrigan said, keeping his voice low. He flexed his clawed hands, a wild light coming into his eyes.

"I bet." He could be an asset, for sure.

But it sounded like at least a half dozen guys were outside. One group on the landing, another down in the street. The two of them against six or seven drifters wasn't good odds. Even with a scrappy fey changeling on her side.

"Come on." The banging on the door intensified. "We know you got cash."

"Begone, foul mortals," Korrigan screeched. "There is nothing here for you."

Marny sent him a sour look. Great. Although it hadn't been likely the drifters would simply leave, the chances of that happening had just evaporated to nothing.

"Some kid," one of the drifters muttered.

"Bring it up," another one said. "We'll beat the door down."

A few seconds later, the door shook with the clang of metal on metal. The drifters had found something large to bash against the door; one of those big metal burn barrels, maybe. If she and Korrigan were lucky, their attackers would only dent the door some, then go away.

But it didn't feel like a lucky night.

Clenching her hands, Marny quickly evaluated their options. She and Korrigan could retreat to the bedroom, maybe get out the window there and climb down the back of the building...

But even if she could squeeze through, the changeling wasn't able to leave the house unless Tam were with him. Dammit. They couldn't escape—so they'd have to fight.

With the constant clashing thud of the drifters at the door as a background, Marny pulled out her old messenger and keyed in a quick call for help.

Not to the police—they'd take too long, if they even came out at all. Tam said the authorities ignored the Exe as much as possible. And she didn't want to risk revealing Korrigan.

:Under attack at Tam's. Help. Bring firepower.:

Uncle Zeg would get her message and be on the way, hopefully with the big flamethrower he'd recently finished rebuilding. Her uncle was worth at least three or four of the drifters, and she knew she could take a couple. Korrigan would pitch in, and they'd repel the attack. They just had to sit tight until Zeg showed up.

She almost messaged Tam, too, but he'd be in-game, and doubtless fighting his own battles. No, she could handle this.

Probably.

"Korr," she said, keeping her voice low, "if they break in, do you have any offensive magic to throw at them? Not the jungle though—it could get in our way."

The changeling gave her one of his horrific grins.

"I can summon any number of nasty crawlies to bite and sting our enemies, should they breach the walls," he said.

"Good. Because I have a feeling things are about to get real."

Not that she thought the drifters would smash through the door, but she'd been keeping an eye on the shadows moving across the wire-webbed living room window. One guy had what looked like a big wooden club, maybe a baseball bat, and it was only a matter of time before he started swinging it at the glass.

She bent and unplugged the cord of the old-fashioned brass lamp on the table by the couch, then stripped the shade off. In this fight, she'd rather swing something heavy at an attacker's head than try to hit a vital spot with a small, pointy object.

The yelling outside intensified, and two of the shadowy

figures turned to the window. One of them lifted his club and swung.

The first crack of wood against glass made Marny wince. No telling how long the window would hold.

"Get ready," she said to Korrigan.

He flexed his spindly, oddly jointed fingers, and nodded.

Another whack, and a spider web of cracks spread across the reinforced glass. It wouldn't be long. She took a deep breath and widened her stance.

The third blow shattered the window, square-edged pieces of safety glass flying into Tam's living room.

"Ha! Told you we could bust it out." The drifter with the wooden club poked at the empty wire, then shoved it aside.

He began to clamber through the wrecked window, but Marny was ready. She brought the lamp down hard on the top of his head, and he crumpled.

"Dude. Why'd you stop?" His companion toed him in the ribs.

A second later, a swarm of weird looking insects poured from around Korrigan and out the widow. Some of them paused to bite and sting the unconscious man, but the rest kept going.

"Hey! Ow! Get off!" the man right outside the window yelled.

Marny glanced at Korrigan. He was mumbling, his fingers moving in strange patterns, his concentration on the insects.

Two more drifters tried to rush the window, which was stupid, because they couldn't both fit through. Marny whacked at them with the base of the lamp. Various cries of pain issued from outside, and one guy ran screaming down the stairs. Still, most of the drifters were not as easily gotten rid of. They'd stopped trying to bang the door down, and turned to the shattered window.

In the distance, Marny heard the loud cough and rattle of a gas car engine, and she smiled through the grimness of battle. Uncle Zeg was on his way. She and Korrigan only needed to hold their attackers off a few moments more.

The gas guzzler pulled up with a screech of brakes loud enough to make the drifters turn. Marny struck the current window-broacher on the shoulder, and Korrigan sent a particularly nasty winged scorpion at his face. The man ducked away, grimacing.

Outside the broken window, a gout of fire lit up the night, reflecting off smoke drifters' yellow-tinged eyes and casting eerie shadows over the dilapidated buildings.

"Want a taste of this?" Zeg's voice called from the street. "I'll give you three seconds to clear out of here, and then things are going to heat up."

Relief surged through Marny, and she tightened her grip on the lamp base. Her uncle was here, and the attackers were toast. Literally.

Two more drifters pelted down the stairs, reached the street, and kept running. The remaining men looked at each other.

"What now, Skeever?" one of them asked, glancing at the man who seemed to be the leader.

"We'll come back later," Skeever. "After this guy leaves."

Marny narrowed her eyes. It was actually a halfway decent plan. Uncle Zeg couldn't protect them for the entire night, after all.

Another blast of fire from the street.

"I'm running out of patience," her uncle called.

"Go." The lead drifter roughly pushed one of his men, and the rest followed.

They ran down the stairs, several of them still swatting at Korrigan's persistent pests. Welts and stings marred their faces and hands, and Marny hoped the bugs had gotten under their clothes, too.

Now that their enemies were fleeing, the adrenaline that had powered her faded, leaving a shaky sadness in its wake.

Tam's house wasn't safe anymore, and her heart wrenched at all the losses he'd been facing. His mom taking off again. His brother stolen by the faeries. And now this.

Uncle Zeg waited until the last drifter ran away into the dark, then, still carrying his flamethrower, slowly backed up the stairs. Marny didn't warn him about the missing seventh stair—she didn't need to. For a big man, her uncle was amazingly light on his feet, and constantly aware of his surroundings. He was pretty much her hero.

Without even looking behind him, he took a giant step backward over the gaping hole.

"You okay up there?" he called softly to them.

"Yeah," Marny said. "Nice timing."

He smiled, teeth white in the dark bush of his beard. "I try."

"Korr, make sure your creatures don't attack my uncle," Marny said.

"They have already returned home," the changeling said.

She didn't ask where home was. Probably some poisonous forest in the heart of the Realm.

"Letting me in?" Uncle Zeg asked from the dented-in door.

Marny set the lamp down, her hand stiff from clutching

the brass base. She snapped on the kitchen light, then went and undid the locks. The metal door opened fine. Too bad the window was wrecked.

Her uncle stood a minute, just looking at her, then set his flamethrower down and enveloped her in a big bear hug. Not many people could do that. She buried her face in his shoulder, smelling smoke and gas fumes.

"Glad you're all right," he said, his voice vibrating through her.

Two wobbly breaths, and she was better.

"Yeah," she said, stepping away. "We're good. Uncle Zeg, meet Korrigan."

She gestured to where the changeling crouched, his bulbous eyes gleaming.

"Charmed," Uncle Zeg said with a nod. He actually meant it, too.

Korrigan blinked, then smiled. "Likewise, mortal man."

As soon as her uncle stepped inside, Marny did up all the locks again.

"I'm letting Tam know what happened," Uncle Zeg said, pulling out his messager.

"Good idea."

She was happy to let her uncle send the message. Her fingers still felt numb from the fight. Plus, she felt too sorry for Tam at the moment for her words to come out right. He didn't need, or want, her sympathy. Life happened, and sometimes you ended on the bottom of the pile. Pity from friends only made it worse.

"He and Roy are on their way," Uncle Zeg said.

"Good." Marny set her hands on her hips and studied the

smashed-out window. "He'll have to move out—at least for a while."

"Yep. Drifters'll be back, and more vicious than ever."

"Good thing your flame thrower works," Marny said.

"Well…" Her uncle's smile was a little sheepish. "The flame part works great. The thrower mechanism leaves a little bit to be desired."

"What? You mean you couldn't have shot fire at the drifters?" She didn't know whether to laugh or cry.

Korrigan nodded in approval. "A show of force is often more impressive than the actuality."

"Then why the crawlies?" Marny asked the changeling. "Why not a big ogre or something?"

"I have no dominion over those kind," Korrigan said. "And I have no desire to be trampled flat beneath enormous feet."

"Fair enough."

"Your insects seemed quite effective," Uncle Zeg said. "From what little I could see."

It was true. Korrigan had come through for them in the fight, in his own peculiar way.

The changeling lifted his head and sniffed the air.

"Tam Linn arrives," he said.

Marny blew out a breath, letting the ache of pity go along with it. Tam would deal, as he always dealt.

She heard his light steps on the creaky stairs, his pause when he saw the broken-out tread, then his quick rush up to the door.

"Guys?" He tapped on the metal. "It's me, Tam."

Zeg undid the locks and opened the door. Tam stepped

in, his expression grim, and Marny decided a big, enveloping hug was the best tactic. After all, it had worked for her.

"Tam," she said, letting go when she felt he was ready.

"Good to see you're ok," he said. "What happened?"

"A couple hours after you and Roy left, we heard someone coming up the stairs. The smoke drifters. They said if we gave them money, they'd go away." She grimaced at the door. "Then they tried to batter down the door."

"We fought them," Korrigan added eagerly. "Mistress Marny laid about with her club, while I sent poisonous crawlies to bite and torment."

"Club?" Tam glanced about, looking for her weapon.

"Yeah," Marny said, pointing her thumb at the lamp. "One guy started coming through the window, so I bashed him. Between that and Korr's bugs, we drove them off. With a little help from Uncle Zeg."

She could see the guilt in Tam's eyes. But it wasn't his fault.

"They haven't come back?" he asked.

"Yet." Uncle Zeg picked up his flame thrower. "But they will. Grab anything important, Tam, anything you want to keep for good. We're clearing you out of here."

For an instant Tam looked lost. "This is my home. I can't just leave."

Marny squeezed his shoulder.

"Where's Roy?" Uncle Zeg asked.

"Waiting with the car," Tam said.

"Now that you are here and can accompany me, we may depart," Korrigan said, oblivious to the undercurrents. He scrambled into the kitchen, hopped onto the counter, and began taking protein bars from the cupboard. "We must take all these. And the screenie system."

Marny felt a wry smile twist her lips. The changeling had his priorities clear, for sure.

"Tam," she said. "It's not secure here anymore." She hated the look in his eyes, but he had to come to grips with the fact his home wasn't a sanctuary any longer.

"But, what if my mom..." He swallowed hard, then continued. "What will Mom think, when she comes home?"

"Leave her a note, and hope the drifters don't mess with it?" There weren't any good solutions.

"You can't stay here." Zeg unplugged the netscreen and began winding up the cords. "I'll take the system down. You go get your stuff."

Tam turned, moving like he was underwater, and started gathering things up—his clothes, a couple books, a battered teddy bear.

He stood there for a moment, arms full of his possessions.

"Here." Marny grabbed one of the blankets off the couch and spread it out, then took the teddy bear and set it in the middle. "Anything from the bedroom?"

"Yeah." He blinked, clearly trying to focus. "Picture album, jewelry box."

"Go get them."

Tam laid the possessions on the blanket, then headed for the bedroom.

"I'll take this lot to the car," Zeg said, arms full of the netscreen setup.

"Good," Marny said.

The sooner they got out of there, the better. She undid the

locks for her uncle, then turned back to the living room. Korr was still rummaging around in the kitchen, filling a plastic bag with protein bars and anything else that caught his eye.

Tam came back out of the bedroom, carrying a few small items and a green dress that probably was his mom's favorite. Wordlessly, he added them to the pile on the blanket, and Marny twisted it up into a bundle.

Uncle Zeg bounded up the stairs and into the living room, his hair wild and frizzy.

"Hurry," he said. "There's something happening at the end of the street."

Probably the smoke drifters gathering. Marny gave Tam a hard look. Whether he was ready or not, they had to go.

Korrigan hopped down from the counter, dragging the plastic bag behind him.

"Let us away," he said, sounding like this was the best adventure ever.

Which, considering he now got to leave the tiny house and see more of the mortal world, it probably was.

"Anything else?" Marny hefted the bundled blanket over her shoulder.

"No," Tam said. "Wait—there's a brand new Zing sim system downstairs."

Uncle Zeg shook his head. "Hopefully the drifters won't think of the shop—or be able to break in. We'll come get it tomorrow."

"Once we repair the window, we can bring everything back," Tam said.

Marny wasn't so sure. The drifters were persistent, and dangerous. It would take more than a few days for them to calm down and slide back into their smoke dreams. Weeks, maybe. And where would Tam live in the meantime?

"Come, come," Korrigan called impatiently.

Through the open door, Marny could hear the rumble of voices borne on the chilly air.

"Marny, ride with me," Uncle Zeg said, starting down the stairs. "Tam, you and the changeling go with Roy."

"But—" Tam started to protest.

"Git 'im!" a rough voice cried from the street. "They're taking the loot!"

"GO!" Zeg shouted, pulling Marny with him down the stairs.

She leaped over the broken tread, and at the bottom of the stairs glanced back at Korrigan. She didn't like to leave him, but he'd be all right with Tam.

"Quick," her uncle said.

Down the block, the drifters were coming toward them, carrying torches. Looked like Uncle Zeg's flamethrower had given them some unfortunate ideas.

"Hey," Roy stuck his head out the window of his grav-car, parked right behind Zeg's guzzler. "What's going on?"

He shot a glance at the approaching drifters, and went pale.

"Start the car," Tam called, clearing the last step.

Marny was glad to see Korrigan right beside him. She sprinted to Uncle Zeg's vehicle and wrenched the passenger door open. It screeched loudly, and the lead drifter, Skeever, lifted his head, his crazed eyes fixing on Marny.

"Over there, ijidts!" he yelled, shaking his torch toward the cars.

The drifters surged forward, their torches leaving oily smears of light against the darkness.

"Get in," Uncle Zeg said, then whirled. "All of you, go!"

"Tam, hurry!" Roy yelled, sliding the passenger-side door open.

Marny buckled in, her fingers clumsy with fear. The drifters were almost on them, dammit. Why was Tam just standing there, staring down the street with that look on his face?

He turned to Uncle Zeg, expression tight with anxiety. And hope.

"My mom's out there," he said. "I have to get her."

Uncle Zeg paused, halfway in the car. "I'll help."

"No. Get Marny out of here. Meet us by The View."

Tam and his drastic heroics. She scowled at him and started to unbuckle her seatbelt.

"Young lady, you stay put," her uncle warned.

He glanced down the street, then, with a low curse, threw himself into the driver's seat and slammed the door. The guzzler started with a coughing roar, and he accelerated forward. The drifters started yelling. One of them grabbed a chunk of concrete from the street and flung it at Roy's car. It left a dent in the shiny red finish.

"We can't just leave Tam," Marny said to her uncle.

"We're not."

Uncle Zeg spun the wheel until they faced back toward the drifters. He thumbed on the high beams, and the mob halted, squinting. Tam picked up Korrigan and threw him into the back of Roy's car, the bag of protein bars clutched to his chest.

The leader of the drifters lunged and grabbed Tam's arm as he got into the grav-car.

"No!" Marny cried.

Uncle Zeg gunned the engine and the guzzler shot forward, but Skeever was already collapsing on the ground. She didn't know what Tam had done, but it had been effective.

Roy's car roared to life, and he skidded around into a U-turn. Sudden alarms and flashing lights split the air, and the drifters milled, confused.

"Roy's car alarm," Uncle Zeg said. "Good move. Now hold on—we're out of here."

"But Tam's mom..."

She watched, heart thumping in her throat, as the grav-car reached a slight figure in a yellow coat. Tam reached out and pulled her into the vehicle.

"They got her. And they'll catch up."

The night cracked again, this time with the sound of a gunshot.

Uncle Zeg accelerated hard, leaving the scorch of burning rubber behind. Marny swiveled in the seat, checking to make sure the red car was behind them.

A searing flash of light made her wince and blink. Then came a chest-rattling *whump* as Tam's house went up in flames. The blue tarp on the roof melted and curled from the gasoline-fueled fire racing over the building. The drifters had brought Molotov cocktails.

And now Tam really had no home to return to. Her eyes burned with smoke, with tears.

Once they got out of the Exe, Uncle Zeg drove quietly, taking the streets that led to The View. Halfway up the final winding road to the compound, he pulled over and killed the engine. The silence of the night pressed in around them.

"So," Uncle Zeg said. "Tell me about the weird creature."

He'd been remarkably calm about encountering Korrigan —but then, he wasn't ruffled by much. And they'd had more pressing issues at the time, like dealing with the smoke drifters.

"That's Korrigan," she said. "Tam's brother was stolen by the faeries, and they left a changeling in his place."

"And you ended up as his babysitter?"

"Someone had to watch the little guy while Tam's in-game."

Uncle Zeg turned in the seat to look at her.

"You didn't feel like mentioning any of this to me?"

Marny shifted with discomfort. "Tell you that faeries are real? Would you have believed it?"

"Yes." His voice was clear with honesty.

"I'm sorry. But everything's been happening so fast." She let out a breath.

"Tam and Jennet's odd character disappearances in the Feyland beta testing aren't just glitches, are they?" he asked.

"No."

She didn't say any more. The fact that Tam and Jennet were entering the Realm was their secret to spill.

Uncle Zeg tapped his fingers on the wheel. "I won't press you, though I suspect tonight will provide some answers."

"What's Tam going to do?" She could voice her worry to Uncle Zeg. "His house is toast—literally."

At least he had his mom, and a few of their most prized possessions.

Uncle Zeg scratched his beard. "The apartment behind my place has been empty since Grandma Tina passed."

"You know Tam won't take charity."

"It's not charity if he works for it. The place needs cleaning up. And he could do some jobs for me at the simcafe too. Don't worry, I'll make it comfortable for him to accept."

Marny nodded with relief. Tam and his family had a place to go. He might be too stubborn to agree on his own behalf, but he'd do it for his mom and the Bug. Provided they got the kid safely out of the Dark Court. Her stomach tightened with worry. What if they couldn't? Tam's life was dire enough without that fear hanging over them like a tornado poised to strike.

Her uncle glanced in the rearview mirror. "Here comes Royal."

Headlights illuminated the inside of the car as Roy pulled up behind them. Marny opened the passenger door, wincing as it squeaked again. She grabbed the blanket filled with Tam's stuff.

The door of Roy's grav-car slid open.

"Special View taxi at your service," Roy said, getting out and waving to the back seat. "Everybody in. We all need to go to Spark's."

"I figured something along those lines," Uncle Zeg said, clambering into the back. "I'm sure the gate guards wouldn't let my car through this time of night."

Tam was in the front seat, his mom on his lap. She looked small and fragile, her gaze unfocused as though she wasn't seeing at the real world at all, but some dream inside her head.

Marny put Tam's bundle on the floor, picked up Korr, and then squeezed in beside Zeg.

"Crowded in here," she said. "And no, Korr, you can't sit on my lap."

He made a face, but didn't protest as she set him down in the middle of the backseat floor. There wasn't much room there, between the bundle, her legs, and Uncle Zeg's, but the changeling would be well hidden from curious humans. Like the guards at the gate.

"We'll be at Spark's in a minute," Roy said, getting back in the car. "Sit tight."

"Like we have any other choice," Marny said.

At least wedged in like this, they wouldn't go flying when Roy took the turns too fast.

The grav-car slid under the plas-metal arch of the view, the guards waving them past without a second glance. Guess the CEO's son could zip in and out any time he liked.

Marny stared at the perfectly landscaped lawns and large houses. The View was so artificial looking. Nobody real lived that way—no toys in the yards, no weeds in the lawn, no character or color anywhere.

"What's the plan?" she asked Tam.

He turned his head, one arm still cradled protectively around his mom. "The beta team has to go in-game to rescue my brother. Tonight. We were going to use the vid Roy made of Korrigan to convince everyone, but..." He shrugged.

"Nothing better than the actual creature," Marny said.

She patted Korrigan on the shoulder. The shape of his bones felt strange under her hand.

It had been a wild night, and was getting wilder. She was thankful she didn't have to sim into Feyland with the team.

There were enough of them that she wouldn't have to force herself onto a sim system—though if she really had to, she would. The thought made her shudder, and she distracted herself by counting up the beta-testing team in her mind: Tam, Jennet, Roy, Uncle Zeg, sim-star Spark Jaxley, and...

"Are you seriously going to ask Jennet's dad to come with you?" she asked.

"We have to." Tam didn't sound happy about it. "We need everyone. And Jennet has been trying to tell him about Feyland for months now. Maybe he'll finally believe her."

Marny hadn't met the man, but he seemed rigid in his opinions.

Then again, they had Korrigan.

"Here we are," Roy said, pulling up to an enormous mansion.

The place rose into the night, at least four stories of glass and steel. Behind the building, the lights of Crestview were spread out like a twinkling blanket. Marny looked, finding the smudge where the Exe glowed with a few sullen lights.

They all piled out of Roy's car, Tam carefully leading his mom, while Korrigan scampered out. For a second, Marny thought the changeling was going to throw himself on the lawn and roll around like a dog, but he managed to restrain himself.

"Okay, everyone—behave." Roy said.

Marny suspected he was mostly talking to Korrigan. And maybe Zeg, who liked to mess with authority. She sent her uncle a half smile, which he returned. No matter how crazy or stressful, this was a prime adventure.

The huge front door swung open at their approach. Probably cameras and sensors all over the place, up here at the top of the compound. A blank-faced security guard stood sentry, and behind him Marny glimpsed a warmly-lit entryway and spacious hall.

"Hi," Roy said. "We'd like to see Spark."

"I'll inform Miss Jaxley you're here," the guard said. "Wait in the great room."

He flicked his gaze to Korrigan, and though his expression didn't change, Marny saw the flicker in his eyes. She hoped Spark's people were discreet.

Roy beckoned them all in, then led the way down the hall, clearly comfortable with the mansion's layout. They passed a table holding a vase full of white lilies, their sweet smell perfuming the air.

What a crazy parade they were. Arrogant gamer boy up front, Tam and his totally spaced-out mom next, Marny after them, trying to keep Korrigan from darting into the side rooms, and Uncle Zeg in the back, big and fuzzy.

The great room was, well, huge. Two-story windows on the far wall looked out over Crestview, the orange city glow washing out the sky above until only a few stars showed through. Tam steered his mom to one of the tan couches at the side of the room. She sat, staring out the window, and Marny hoped she wasn't completely lost. Surely she was inside there, somewhere, and would wake up soon.

Uncle Zeg stood by the door, and Marny took her place beside him. Neither of them wanted to make themselves comfortable. Not until they knew what was going on, and where they fit in.

Roy grinned at Korrigan. "Take a seat," he said, pointing to the big couch in the center of the room.

Obviously he wanted the changeling to make an impression the second Spark walked in.

Korrigan gave him a toothy smile, then hopped up and squatted on the plush upholstery. He looked wild and matted and dangerous, incongruous in the middle of the fancy mortal trappings. Give him a carnivorous forest, or a treacherous stream, and he'd be right at home.

Did he miss the Realm? It was hard to tell, he was such an irascible creature, but Marny thought maybe he did, despite the lure of protein bars. Certainly he didn't belong in the human world.

Brisk footsteps approached, and Spark Jaxley appeared at the door. In person, she looked just as prime as the gaming posters featuring her image—same bright magenta hair, same intent, intelligent gaze.

She paused and raised one eyebrow when she saw them all gathered in the room. Then her gaze found Korrigan, and the other brow rose.

"Well," she said. "This is interesting."

The changeling stood, his clawed feet gripping the couch, and made her a bow.

"Well met, milady," he said in his scratchy voice.

"I take it you're not from around here," Spark said.

Marny pursed her lips in approval of the gamer girl's calm reaction.

"He's from Feyland," Tam said. "I know it's hard to believe, but the game connects our world to the Realm of Faerie. Which, as you can see, is real."

Spark's mouth firmed, her eyes narrowed in thought. "There have been some strange things in that game, I'll admit. Things not even prime-level programming could achieve. So does this mean that faeries are overrunning the earth? Should we be freaking out?"

"Not yet," Tam said. "But things might get dire."

Zeg leaned forward, absorbing Tam's words.

"What are we going to do about it?" Uncle Zeg asked. "I presume the beta team is going in-game. Then what?"

"Then we hope we get lucky," Roy said, a twinge of bitterness in his voice. "Tam and Jennet have apparently managed to score an epic sword and talk to the guardians between the realms, or something like that."

Tam gave Roy a serious look. "It wasn't all fun and games."

"Speaking of Jennet," Spark glanced around, "where is she?"

Spark slowly walked around the couch, keeping an eye on Korrigan, and then leaned against the back. Marny moved into the room, too. No point in standing around awkwardly, now that it was clear Spark wasn't going to throw them out.

"Jennet should be on her way over," Tam said. "With her dad."

"Her dad?" The surprise was clear in Spark's voice.

"There's no other way for us to get into VirtuMax headquarters and onto the sim systems," Tam said. "We need Mr. Carter's help—and his access codes."

"Like Zeg said, then what?" Spark asked.

"We'll make a plan," Tam said. "As soon as they get here."

"We're here," Jennet said from the doorway.

She glanced at Korrigan still crouching on the plush tan couch, then swallowed and looked back at her dad. Marny mentally crossed her fingers. She'd never met Jennet's dad, but his actions spoke plenty loud.

"What the hell is that?" Mr. Carter stopped, one foot over the threshold. His expression was a mixture of confusion and revulsion as he stared at the changeling.

Marny studied Korrigan. She'd gotten used to, and a little fond of, his bulbous eyes, the slash of his mouth filled with sharp teeth, and the unlikely arrangement of his limbs. But he was still a revolting, otherworldly creature.

"That," Tam said, "is a changeling from the Unseelie Court of the Realm of Faerie."

"I..." Jennet's dad blinked, clearly having problems processing what he was seeing.

Uncle Zeg stepped forward, his voice sympathetic. "Hard to take in, I know. I've seen a lot of things in my life, but this is one of the strangest."

"Is it real?" Mr. Carter took a few hesitant steps into the room.

Korrigan narrowed his eyes, unhappy that his existence was in doubt.

"Shall I conjure up my crawlies, the better to convince you?" he asked crankily.

"No need," Marny said quickly, shaking her head. "You're proof enough, Korr. Plus, your bugs are hideous."

If Jennet's dad saw the weird nightmarish creatures, he'd probably run screaming out the door. Better to take things slowly for now.

"Can I... touch it?" Mr. Carter asked.

He approached the changeling, one hand out. Marny wanted to warn him it was a bad idea; but then again, letting Korr be himself was the best way to convince Jennet's dad of his reality.

With a hiss, the changeling swiped his thick black claws

out, catching the sleeve of Mr. Carter's jacket. Korrigan pulled, and Jennet's dad stumbled over to stand face-to-face with the faerie. The rasp of Mr. Carter's breathing was loud in the watching silence.

"Close enough, mortal?" Korrigan bared his teeth.

"Let him go." Marny stepped up, ready to interfere if things got nasty.

It was one thing to prove he was real, but there was a line she couldn't allow Korr to cross. No injuries. Either to fey creatures or human allies.

The changeling grimaced unhappily, but pulled his claws free and released Jennet's dad. Mr. Carter took three hasty steps back. His face was pale, and a drop of sweat trickled down from his temple.

"All right," he said, pulling down the sleeve of his jacket. "I believe you."

About time, too.

"Finally," Tam said, echoing Marny's thoughts.

Jennet's dad studied Korrigan a moment longer, then rubbed his face.

"I owe you an apology," he said, turning to where Jennet stood beside Tam. "To both of you. Honey, I... you have to understand how impossible your stories sounded, I thought you were making up wild excuses."

Jennet crossed her arms, a stubborn look on her face, and Marny didn't blame her. A single apology wouldn't erase months of issues.

"This would have been a lot simpler if you'd believed me in the first place," she said.

"I know." To his credit, Mr. Carter sounded genuinely sorry.

"Hey." Uncle Zeg, always the peacemaker, clapped his hand on Mr. Carter's shoulder. "We all make mistakes. The thing is to keep moving forward. Speaking of which, it's getting late, and we have plans to make."

From what Marny had gathered about the beta testing, the two adults had spent some time questing together. They seemed an unlikely pair, but then again, stranger things had happened.

She glanced at Korrigan. He still looked grumpy. With a wink, she tossed him one of the foil-wrapped protein bars she'd grabbed from his stash.

Although he scowled at her, he deftly caught it.

"Zeg's right," Spark said. "Everybody, sit down. We need to sort things out."

Roy, of course, immediately sprawled in the most comfortable-looking chair. "I'm thinking we wait until after midnight to sneak into headquarters, in case anyone's working late."

Tam and Jennet moved to the small sofa, and Marny settled into one of the double-wide armchairs. Uncle Zeg followed her lead. Nobody sat next to Korrigan.

"I'll ask the cook to throw together some pizzas," Spark said. "No commando raids on an empty stomach."

Marny agreed. When was the last time she had eaten? Or Tam, for that matter—the boy was always hungry.

"Ok." Tam leaned forward, resting his elbows on his knees. "You've all met Korrigan. He's the changeling that..." He glanced over at his mom, who seemed entranced by the lights of Crestview sparkling below.

Tam swallowed, then continued. "The changeling that was left in place of my brother."

"I don't understand," Mr. Carter said.

"Dad," Jennet said, "the Dark Court faeries stole Tam's little brother and are keeping him hostage. Our job tonight is to rescue him."

"Let me see if I have this right," Uncle Zeg said. "The game of Feyland actually leads to fairyland—which is a real, magical place?"

Marny knew that her uncle understood—he'd gotten it right away. But clearly Mr. Carter was still a little lost. Didn't hurt to restate things for his benefit. Especially since they needed him on their side in order to enter VirtuMax's super-secure headquarters and log on to the beta-test sim systems.

"Yes," Tam said.

"That'll be something to see." Her uncle's brown eyes gleamed with interest. "So, we go in-game, find this Dark Court place, and rescue Tam's little brother."

"Except it won't be that easy," Roy said, showing a rare flash of good sense.

Spark nodded. "I assume we're in for an epic battle."

"Yeah." There was the bare edge of worry in Tam's voice. "Thing is, there are two courts, and apparently they've joined forces."

"So this is a bad thing?" Zeg asked.

"Extremely." Tam sat up straight. "Which is why we need everyone's help. Jennet and I can't defeat the king and queen, not by ourselves."

Roy made a noise, and Tam shot him a look. "Not the three of us either, Roy. You don't know what the Dark Queen is like."

Marny knew that Tam and Jennet, working together, had barely beaten the Dark Queen in battle once before. And that, with the addition of Roy, they'd managed to escape the Bright King's court. But Tam was right—if the two fey monarchs were working together, the humans would need all the help they could get.

After consuming the better part of five pizzas, the beta team had their plan of attack. Two plans, really. The first involved sneaking into VirtuMax, and the second was how to proceed in-game once they were in Feyland.

Marny didn't say much, just munched her olive and pepperoni slice and kept an eye on Korrigan. He seemed partial to the all-veggie pizza, which surprised her a little. Then again, she didn't really want to know what his idea of a gourmet meal was. Worms and dirt, probably. Raw fish.

Tam was feeding his mom pieces of cheese pizza. She was still in a daze, but maybe the food would help. Marny went to join him on the side couch.

"What's your mom's first name?" she asked.

It was obvious to her, if not everyone else, that she'd be staying at Spark's to look after Korrigan and Tam's mom. But if something went wacky, she wasn't sure the woman would answer to "Mrs. Linn." And definitely not to "hey, Tam's mom!"

"It's Lara," Tam said, a little catch in his voice.

Jennet laid her hand on his knee. "She'll be all right."

"Maybe." Tam took his mom's unresisting hand and turned it, holding her wrist to the light. "Do you see that?"

Marny squinted and leaned forward. Despite her fear

she'd be looking at drug-related marks, the only thing on Lara's skin was a pattern of silvery dots. Almost like...

"A faerie handprint?" Jennet asked.

"Yeah. My mom said a 'shining girl' talked to her tonight, and told her to come home. I don't know if it was a malicious faerie, or one trying to help." He shivered.

"Good thing you got her out of there," Marny said. "Before—"

She made herself stop. The last thing Tam needed was a reminder that his home was now a burned-out shell.

"Okay!" Spark called, standing up and stretching her hands. "Are we ready to do this?"

Jennet glanced at her dad, who had set aside his half-eaten slice of Canadian bacon and pineapple. He nodded and stood.

"I suppose so," he said.

Tam rose, his worried gaze focused on his mom. "Stay here with Marny," he said. "I'll be back in a while."

His mom smiled at him, her expression still dreamy and unfocused. It was hard to know if she even understood what he was saying.

"Take care of her," he said to Marny. It was more a plea than a command.

"No worries," she said.

That was her, Marny Fanalua; babysitter to changeling creatures and zoned-out moms. Still, it was better than squeezing into a sim chair and enclosing herself in the stifling helmet. Even the thought of it made her throat scratchy with rising panic. Nope, small spaces and her didn't get along at all.

"Ready?" Uncle Zeg asked in his calm, rumbling voice.

For a half second, Marny wanted to jump up and grab his arm, beg him not to put himself and her friends in danger. But they had to go. It was what heroes did.

The rest of the beta team nodded and started moving to the door.

"Good luck," Marny said. "I'll keep an eye on things here."

Tam turned and pointed at Korrigan. "Stay in this building, and do what Marny tells you."

Marny raised her brows. The changeling would certainly do the first, and definitely not the second. But that was okay —she had a few more protein bars in her pocket.

Spark gave her tight smile. "If you need anything, ask my staff. I've told them you have the run of the place."

"We'll probably just hang out in this room," Marny said. She didn't want to go chasing Korrigan through a five-story mansion.

"There's a vidscreen on the left wall. The painting slides down and the controls are there." Spark pointed. "And tell the house if you want something sent up from the kitchen."

"Will do. Now go kick some faerie butt," Marny said. Korrigan squawked, and she sent him an exasperated look. "Present company excepted, of course."

Uncle Zeg gave her a big hug, and Jennet a more diminutive one. Tam squeezed her shoulder and she squeezed his in return, Roy sent her a jaunty salute, Spark waved, and Mr. Carter just looked stressed.

Then they were gone, trooping down the hall and out into the chilly night. The big mansion seemed way too quiet. Marny tried to ignore the little flare of jealousy that all her friends were going off to fight while she remained on babysitting duty. Epic battles were their thing, not hers.

Don't you think you're good enough? a voice inside her whis-pered. You're a better gamer than Roy. A better person.

Yeah, well. She might be both those things, but she was still plain old Marny. Not a brilliant gamer like Tam, or a brave rich-girl like Jennet. Not even a CEO's spoiled kid. Just an ordinary girl, who took up a little extra space in the world.

She let out a breath, then stepped back into the room and closed the door. It might be a "great room," but compared to the enormous expanse of the rest of the house, it felt down-right cozy

Korrigan was rooting around in the leftover pizza. Tomato sauce made his claws look bloody.

"Are you done eating?" Marny asked.

"There is no more of the delicious kind left." The changeling frowned.

"Then let's get you cleaned up."

There was a lavish bathroom attached to the great room, of course. There was probably a bathroom for every room in the place. Before taking Korrigan in, she glanced at Tam's mom, but Lara seemed fine, caught up in some reverie only she could see.

"What is this?" Korrigan hopped into the big bathtub, then rapped on the sides. "A bin to put treasure in?"

"No. You fill it with water to bathe in. Like a little pond. And before you ask, I'm not running you a bath." Seeing Korrigan without his tunic and trousers would probably scar her for life.

He didn't press the point, which was good, though he did splash water from the sink all over the floor. Marny mopped it up with one of the thick cream-colored towels. The smell of floral soap perfumed the air.

When they went back into the other room, Marny was relieved to see that Lara hadn't moved.

"Let us kart race," Korrigan said, scrambling up to the back of the couch and giving Marny a hopeful look.

"I don't think there's a screenie system in here," Marny said.

"Then find one," the changeling demanded.

Marny shook her head. She wasn't going to impose on Spark's hospitality. And she had a feeling that asking the staff to accommodate a grumpy fey creature like Korrigan and get him set up for gaming would be too much.

"We can watch some vids, though," she said, heading over to the wall.

The control panel was right where Spark had said. Marny hit the button to activate the vidscreen, and the image of a newscaster appeared. Boring. She scrolled through the channels.

"See anything you like?" she asked.

"Yes! There." Korrigan pointed to the channel where a lion chased gazelles over the dry African plains.

They probably didn't have lions in the Realm of Faerie, but if they did, she could imagine Korrigan trying to take one down. Or tame it. The thought made her smile.

Once she got the changeling settled in front of the screen, she went over to Tam's mom. Maybe some contact with the real world would help her come back from whatever dream-land she seemed to be inhabiting.

"Hey, Lara." Marny sat down beside Tams' mom, who didn't turn her gaze from the window. "What are you looking at?"

"All the pretty lights. And wings," Lara said softly, rubbing the silver marks on her wrist.

Marny leaned forward and peered out the window. It was hard to see past the flickering reflection of carnage on the savannah.

There—a flicker of gossamer wings. A scattering of sparks moving through the sky.

"Um, Korr?" Marny said. "Do you see anything interesting outside?"

The changeling glanced out the window, then shrugged. "Only the pixies and faerie maids."

She swallowed. "You mean creatures from the Realm are flying around out there?"

"They are boring, insipid creatures," Korrigan said. "Lions are of far more interest."

"To you, maybe." Marny stood and moved to the window, letting her shadow cut the light from the room so she could see out more clearly. "Why are they there?"

"The boundary between the worlds is thinning," the changeling said. "I can feel the fey magic seeping out."

"Is this because of the beta team going in-game?"

"Perchance. Or because, with my presence in your world and the mortal boy's in the Dark Court, the connection here is strong. This city is becoming a nexus, where the two worlds may more easily overlap."

She didn't like the sound of that.

From the darkness outside, a faerie maiden suddenly swooped close to the glass. She was about as tall as Marny, but thin as a handful of sticks. Pale wings protruded from her back, flapping slowly. As they caught the light they shimmered, opalescent. Tam's mom let out a sigh.

"So pretty," she said.

Yeah, until you looked closely and saw the sharp teeth, the alien consciousness in those pupil-less eyes. Marny shivered. The team better rescue Tam's brother, and help stop whatever was letting fey creatures through into their world.

"Do we have to worry about anything dangerous getting loose?" Marny asked.

She made shooing motions at the faerie, but the creature hovered in place outside the window, staring at her. Creepy.

"Unlikely," Korrigan said over the cries of dying gazelles. "The gateway is not big enough to allow more than the lesser fey folk through."

"Let's hope that doesn't change." She squeezed her hands into fists. The beta team had better succeed.

Fewer things were worse than waiting around, powerless. The next few hours were going to crawl by.

"Gah!" Korrigan's strangled call made Marny turn.

He was lying on the plush carpet, pinned there by two small, squat creatures even uglier than he was. One of them raised a sharpened wooden spear.

"Stop!" Marny yelled.

Adrenaline jolting through her, she bent and whipped out her knife, then dashed around the couch and shoved Korrigan's attacker away. The blade touched the creature's leathery skin, and it hissed in pain and retreated a few steps.

"Get off him," she warned, waving her knife at the one still holding Korrigan down.

It scowled at her, eyes full of malice, and slowly released the changeling. Korrigan scuttled back on all fours, then stopped and raised his hands.

"Begone, foul hobgoblins," he screeched. "Before I drive you forth with stings and bites."

The one holding the spear growled and shook it at Korrigan, but Marny put herself between it and the changeling.

"You heard him." She pointed her knife at the hobgoblins. "Or do you need more convincing?"

With a last, evil glare, the creatures muttered something that might have been a spell. Purple light flared, and Marny put up her arm to shield her eyes. When she lowered it, there was no sign of the hobgoblins. Her heart was pounding, the beat a steady thump, thump in her ears.

"Are they really gone?" She turned to Korrigan.

"Aye." He winced. "Kindly put away your blade, Mistress Marny. The cold iron burns the air."

"Right. Sorry."

She remembered Jennet telling her that the fey folk couldn't abide the touch of iron. Another good reason to carry her knife, evidently.

Marny glanced at where Tam's mom sat. The woman seemed oblivious to what had just happened, and was still staring out the window. At least the freaky faerie maiden was gone.

Korrigan let out a grunt and got to his feet.

"Are you okay?" Marny slid her knife back in her leg sheath, then hurried to his side. "Did they hurt you?"

"They meant to." He grimaced. "The queen sent them to kill me."

"But if you're injured while in the mortal world..." Realization iced her bones. "The queen wanted Tam's brother to die."

"A human's death in the Realm of Faerie carries great

power. She still intends to sacrifice the child, but it will be more difficult now that your friends have entered the Realm."

"Wait, what? How do you know?" Marny had to raise her voice over the sound of roaring lions, and quickly muted the vid. A little too much excitement going on without the addition of the brutal soundtrack.

Korrigan looked affronted. "I am a creature of the Realm. I am aware of what transpires there, even from my entrapment here in the human world."

"Then tell me what's happening," she said. "The beta team can't have gotten there already."

"Time moves differently in the Realm," he said. "Your mortal friends are approaching the Dark Court."

"I want you to tell me everything you can. What exactly they're doing in there, how the battle is going, all of it."

Korrigan screwed up his face and grunted. Was this the prelude to a changeling tantrum?

"Look," he said, waving at the vidscreen.

The image was blurry, and strobing light/dark/light, but Marny could make out a group of characters gathered at a crossroads. On the hill above them rose a circle of standing stones, illuminated with eerie purple light.

"Is that the beta team?" she asked, squinting to see the figures.

"Aye." Korrigan sounded a little breathless. "And see, the Faerie Rade approaches."

They looked like an army—elfin knights in shining silver armor, redcap goblins capering behind, brandishing their wickedly sharp blades. Rank after rank of faerie folk, and in the center a woman astride a tall horse, with a crown of stars blazing upon her brow.

It was like watching some epic fantasy movie—except that this was really happening, to people she cared about.

The odds didn't look good. Marny crossed her arms, trying to breathe out her anxiety. Worry wouldn't help her friends, and would only tweak her out.

The image wavered, then disappeared. She was staring at lions again, now hunting a zebra.

"Hey!" She turned to Korrigan.

"The connection is difficult to sustain," he said. "As I told you before, time is not parallel between our worlds. I am doing my best."

It was true the changeling seemed tired, his brow furrowed and his skin even paler than usual.

"Okay," Marny said. "Don't hurt yourself. But if you can get the picture back at some point, that would be great."

He nodded. "Another moment of rest, and I will try once more."

"Have a protein bar." She handed him the last one in her pocket.

Judging by how quickly he ripped the wrapper off and devoured it, channeling the Realm of Faerie was hungry work.

When he was finished, he narrowed his eyes and stared at the vidscreen.

The African plains dissolved and the Realm came back, a little distorted. Marny leaned forward, worry crashing through her. The beta-team members had been taken captive, and were tied to different standing stones at the top of the hill. They were all in a state of bad to even worse. Marny sucked in her breath at the sight of one slumped figure who looked almost dead.

"Is that Mr. Carter's character?"

"Aye."

Uncle Zeg was tied to the next stone, and Marny breathed a prayer of thanks that he was upright. He glared at the two figures standing in the center of the circle—the Dark Queen and what must certainly be the Bright King. Red and blue flames coruscated between them—

The image shivered, shifted, and now Marny saw Tam's little brother being held by the king. The fey monarch lifted a needle-sharp blade. Both Zeg and Tam rushed forward, and behind them, Jennet sliced her own radiant sword down—

A huge black dragon hovered in the sky above the standing stones. It lifted its head, its gaze piercing, and Marny swore those centuries-deep eyes looked directly at her and Korrigan. She shivered. The dragon brought its ebony wings together in a thunderclap—

The vidscreen went dark, and Korrigan crumpled to his knees.

"Korr!" Marny went to her own knees at his side, and gently lifted him.

He felt nearly hollow, all knobbles and bone in her arms. His pale, bulging eyes blinked up at her, and he gave her a crooked smile.

"Mistress Marny, do not fear for me," he croaked.

"Is Tam's brother dying? Are you? What's happening?" She wanted to shake him for answers, but he seemed suddenly so breakable.

"The guardians between the worlds have been called," he said. "I am being pulled back to the Realm."

"Are you sure it won't kill you?" Her heart was pounding, but there was nothing she could do.

"The transition is... difficult. But I will survive."

"Does that mean the Bug is coming back to the real world?" A whoosh of relief temporarily displaced her fear, and her eyes stung with hope. With dismay.

"He will arrive here shortly," Korrigan said. "And now I must bid you farewell."

Unexpected sadness pierced her heart. "Will I ever see you again?"

Who knew that she'd become so fond of this weird, aggravating little creature? She was glad he'd managed to beat her in their last kart race. A small victory to leave the human world with.

"Our paths have tangled and twined," he said. "And the Elder has gazed into your eyes. The mark of the fey folk will be upon you now, and who knows where that might lead?"

Probably no place good.

But certainly guaranteed not to be boring.

"Take care of yourself," she said, blinking to clear her vision of tears.

"And you, mortal girl. I am happy to have called you my companion."

He grimaced, even as his body started to fade. He grew lighter and lighter in her arms, until at last she was holding only empty air.

"Goodbye, Korr," she whispered, bowing her head.

A flash of light, and something heavy landed on her, knocking her nearly off balance. She ducked a wild kick, and grabbed at the arm flailing around in front of her face. The Bug had arrived back in the real world.

"Hey, hey," she said, doing her best to channel Uncle Zeg's super-zen manner. "Calm down. It's okay—you're back."

The Bug looked up at her, eyes like Tam's in a younger, more mischievous face. He froze for a second, then bent over and started crying.

Marny hoisted him up and took him to the couch where Lara sat. Or had been sitting. She was standing now, her eyes looking more awake, her arms outstretched.

"Is that my boy?" she said, her voice strained. "Peter?"

"Mom?" The Bug lifted his wet, snotty face. "Mom!"

Before Marny could tighten her grip, he'd launched himself from her arms and tackled his mom. Luckily the plush sofa was right behind them, catching them as they went down. Tam's mom was crying too, and rubbing her son's hair.

"I'll grab some tissues," Marny said, retreating to the bathroom to give them some privacy.

She couldn't guess how aware Lara had been of Korrigan's presence. Weren't changelings glamoured so everyone believed they were the replaced child? Yet clearly Tam's mom could see the fey folk. Maybe her shutting down had more to do with an inability to believe the enchantment trying to tell her Korrigan was her own son, when he was obviously a hideous-looking fey creature.

Marny might do the same, if half her brain wanted her to believe an ugly, foul-tempered alien creature was actually her beloved kid. She'd been taken in by glamour before, and frankly, it was impressive that Lara had managed to sidestep it. Even if it had made her practically a vegetable.

"Where's Tam?" The Bug's high-pitched voice carried into the bathroom.

Marny came out with a handful of tissues and handed

them to Lara. She took them, then started wiping her son's face.

"Tam should be here soon," Marny said, though she wasn't at all certain of the fact.

Sure, Korrigan had returned to the Realm and the Bug had made it home to the human world. But that didn't necessarily mean everyone on the beta team was all right. Or even alive.

She swallowed, refusing to entertain the idea for more than a second. Whatever that big dragon had been, she didn't think it would let any of her friends die.

She hoped.

"I'll get the staff to bring up some hot tea," Marny said.

"And cookies?" Tam's little brother lifted his head hopefully.

"If they have any."

For a kid who had just spent two weeks in the Dark Court, the Bug was bouncing back remarkably well.

She stepped into the hall to summon one of Spark's security guys, but paused at the sound of voices in the foyer.

"Bug?" It was Tam's voice, echoing down the hall.

Quick as a thought, Tam's little brother pushed past Marny and pelted toward the front door, footsteps slapping against the marble floor.

"Tam!" he cried.

Marny smiled as the Bug ran into Tam's arms, then smiled even wider as his mom ran forward. Lara paused in front of her boys, and placed her hand on Tam's shoulder. Without looking up, he pulled her into the embrace.

Beyond them, Marny saw Jennet watching, a look of such tenderness and joy on her face that Marny's heart stung. Tam seemed to feel Jennet's gaze on him, and lifted his head. Their gazes met, and Marny could practically see the light moving between them.

Maybe one day she would have that. She didn't know how, or when, or if Korrigan had been right that there were more fey adventures in her future.

Only way to find out was to keep moving ahead one moment, one day at a time.

Meanwhile, there was Uncle Zeg, and the bulwark of his embrace. She leaned into him and let the tight string of worry wrapping around her go.

"You won?" she asked, though she knew the answer.

"Yes." He smiled down at her, teeth white behind his fuzzy beard. "We won."

That was all anyone could ask for. It was enough to keep the world turning—and the faeries at bay for another day.

THE BUG IN THE DARK COURT

CHAPTER 1

PETER LINN—THE Bug to most everybody who knew him—
yawned and burrowed deeper into his sleeping bag. He'd
heard his brother, Tam, leave for high school, and then his
mom go out, but she hadn't made him wake up, and he was
good with that.

Third grade was boring. And hard. Which was tweaked,
that it could be both those things without much fun in the
middle, but there it was. He was glad to stay home by himself.
Nobody around to make him stop at two bowls of Sugar
Crunchies, or turn down the music, or shut off the screenie
games because they thought he was playing too much.

He wished he could go downstairs to the abandoned
garage, and try out Tam's sim-chair and games—but that was
strictly off limits. Plus, the door was triple-locked. He knew
'cause he'd tried to get in for hours that one time, when Tam
was out with his friends.

The thought of Sugar Crunchies got Bug moving. He
kicked his sleeping bag to the side and went barefoot into the
kitchen. No point in changing out of his jammies—which

were just an old T-shirt and a pair of sweats. Pretty much what we would have put on for the day, anyway.

He flipped the power on the squat oval of the Holler sitting on the counter, which was tuned to his favorite band, Zangclang. The room immediately filled with the pulsing drumbeats of *Crush It*, the best song ever written. Bug sang along with the chorus as he poured out a huge bowl of Sugar Crunchies.

"*We gonna rock it til the break of daaaay.*" He wailed the word along with the lead singer, although he always ran out of breath before Zangclang did. "*No need to rush it, rush it...*"

Carrying his cereal in both hands, Bug danced back into the living room. The final words of the song made him laugh as he sang to his bowl of Sugar Crunchies.

"*Oh baby, then we crush it!* Yeah, I'm gonna crush you, breakfast."

Still grinning, he settled down in the nest of his sleeping bag. It was a good morning, and getting better. While he ate, he'd power up the flatscreen and play a couple rounds of kart racing. Then maybe switch to that cooking game. It was for little kids, and mostly dumb, but he'd figured out how to glitch it by combining ingredients that weren't supposed to go together, and that was fun.

He pointed the controller at the screen and was about to start gaming when something weird started happening in the middle of the room. Like there was a light shining from the other side of the air, and dim shapes moving around in whatever that place was.

The skin on the back of his neck prickled. Slowly, he set his half-eaten bowl of Sugar Crunchies aside.

"Hello?" he said.

The strange spot bulged, like something was pushing to get through. Bug gripped the game controller tightly. Maybe he could whack whatever emerged on the head. His breath felt itchy, and he wished with all his heart that Tam was there.

There was a bright flash of light, and he flinched away, his ears popping like he'd swallowed wrong.

"Hark," a high, piping voice said from inside the light. "We have arrived. Cease thy cringing, Korrigan, and see what the current mortal world holds."

The brightness faded, revealing two small monster-guys. Bug didn't yell, because they weren't huge, but his heart slammed against his ribs. He blinked a couple times, hoping it was just a funny dream, but no. They were there, all right, standing on the grubby carpet at the edge of the couch.

The one closest to him had bulgy eyes with white centers, and really sharp teeth. The other one... Bug let out a relieved breath and loosened his deathly grip on the controller.

He recognized the bright-eyed little guy in a dress made of dried leaves. That was a faerie-dude, and had something to do with Tam, and sim games, and Bug wasn't sure what all else.

"Hey, Puck," he said. "Um, whatcha' doing? Tam's not here."

"Greetings, Peter-known-as-Bug," the faerie-dude said. "We have not arrived for your brother, but for you."

A tingle—half fear, half excitement—went through Bug. Finally, he got to be the one having adventures!

"This?" The ugly creature turned to Puck, sounding annoyed. "This whey-faced human boy? He is too old."

Puck rose up into the air, so that he was looking down at the creature.

It was a really prime trick. Bug squinted his eyes and imagined he was floating—but no luck. His bare feet stayed firmly planted on the rug.

"Bide, Korrigan," Puck said. "Are you not the best dissembler among your kind? You have been chosen due to the very difficulty of this assignment. Indeed, no one but yourself would have a hope of succeeding."

The creature, Korrigan or whatever, grinned an ugly grin, his thin lips stretched over sharp yellow teeth.

"True, true," he said, satisfaction in his whiny voice.

He stepped forward, clawed hands outstretched, and Bug skipped back a nervous pace. He glanced at Puck.

"Is this guy gonna eat me or something?"

Puck laughed, a sound like wind chimes, and turned a somersault in midair. "Have no fear, youngling. He seeks only to learn your form, so that he might mimic your appearance."

"Um." Bug sidled behind the small table where his family took their meals. "Why?"

"So that you may come on a grand journey with me," Puck said. "How does a bit of adventure sound?"

"Good?" Bug wasn't sure though. He trusted Puck—well, kinda. But this Korrigan guy was freaky. "Won't Tam notice I'm gone?"

The ugly creature snorted. "Thus my presence, foolish human child. I shall take your place."

"Oh." Bug rubbed his foot against the back of his leg.

"We shall not be gone long." Puck swooped close, hovering over the tabletop. "Worry not."

He held out his hand.

Bug pushed his mouth into a frown. This felt kinda tweaked. But also magical. Maybe magic *was* tweaked, which was why he had little prickles running all through him. He looked at the figure floating before him, leaves tangled in his hair, a spark of laughter in his bright eyes.

"Okay," Bug said. "I guess I'll come."

"Excellent." Puck nodded, his grin widening. "Korrigan, complete your transformation."

The ugly creature bounded over to Bug and lightly brushed his black claws down Bug's arm. Bug looked down, but it didn't hurt, and his skin wasn't scratched or anything.

A second later, Korrigan began to change, like something out of a vid. His eyes shrunk, his skin turned pale, and his squat body grew skinny. A moment later, a human boy with messy brown hair and a smudge on one cheek stood facing Bug.

"Is that me?" He scooted out from behind the table so he could go around and see himself from behind. "That's prime. How come the back of my head looks weird?"

Korrigan let out an annoyed growl, and the strange lumpiness on the back of not-Bug's head smoothed out.

"Are you ready?" Puck held his hand out to Bug.

"Make sure you finish the Sugar Crunchies," Bug told the creature that looked like him. "And don't talk. Especially to my mom."

Korrigan smiled, a nasty smile that looked weird on Bug's own face. "She will not be a concern."

"What do you mean?" Bug leaned forward, his hands folding into fists. "If you hurt her—"

"Fret not, child," Puck said. "Korrigan only means that we shall be gone and back again 'ere your family has a chance to discover your absence. Now set your hand in mine, for our journey is about to commence."

Heart fluttering like that bird that got trapped inside the living room one time, Bug reached over and touched Puck's warm palm. The faerie closed his fingers over Bug's.

"Do not fear," Puck said. "The crossing will be uncomfortable, but not dangerous."

"Where are we going, anyway?"

The faerie gave him a look that seemed a little sad. "The Dark Court, child. You are going to meet the Queen."

CHAPTER 2

A FLASH of golden light made Bug blink, and he had a queasy sensation in his stomach. He felt like he was falling but also flying, and for a second he could taste the color of the air. Puck's grasp was the only solid thing in the world. Or between the worlds

Then they landed with a silent thump, and the faerie let go of his hand.

"We have arrived," Puck said solemnly.

It was dark, and it took a second for Bug's eyes to adjust to the dimness. They were outside, in a clearing surrounded by tall trees with crooked branches that were blacker shadows against the starry sky. The air was warm and filled with strange voices speaking a language he could *almost* understand.

A purple fire on one side of the clearing shed some light, as did the fingernail paring of a crescent moon overhead, and after a few moments, Bug could see better. The cool, springy stuff he was standing on turned out to be moss, and he dug his bare toes into it, trying to feel if it was real or just a rug.

He and Puck faced a throne made of twisted black roots. Sitting on the throne was a lady, but not like anybody from his world. She had a pointy face with scary eyes, and pointy ears, too. Her skin was as pale as the cracked china plate in the cupboard, and her hair was like a black cloud with fireflies caught in the storm.

Behind the throne stood skinny girls with misty dresses and shimmering wings who watched him with wide eyes. Other creatures clustered around the queen lady, and they didn't look as pretty as the faerie girls or as nice as Puck. Short ugly dudes with sharp teeth and red hats nudged each other and cackled. Something that was maybe an ogre stood in the shadows, a big club in one hand.

Greenish blobs of light floated through the warm air, like ugly lights. Or maybe they were creatures—it was hard to tell. One trailed past and Bug wrinkled his nose at the stench.

"Your highness." Puck bowed to the lady on the throne. "I have brought you the human child, as requested."

The pale-dark queen leaned forward, and a cold breeze tickled the back of Bug's neck. She studied him intently. After a second, he shifted his gaze to the mossy ground in front of the throne. Whatever lurked in her crazy, magical eyes, he didn't want it to catch him.

"Mortal boy," she said, her voice sounding like moonlight, if moonlight talked. "Welcome to the Dark Court. We are delighted to have you visit."

The gathered creatures tittered, and Bug frowned. He could tell they were bullies just waiting to trip him or poke him or steal his treats. The thing to do was to ignore them, really. But that might not be so easy, since he couldn't just go home from wherever the Dark Court was.

"Okay," he said.

Her pale fingers curled over the gnarled wood of her throne. "What is your name?"

A thick silence fell, and Bug could tell the answer was important. He breathed in slow, through his nose, then out through his mouth.

The air grew colder as the lady waited for his reply.

"Peter," he finally said. It was true—but it also wasn't his name. Not really. He was the Bug.

"Excellent." She stood, a satisfied note in her voice, and raised her pale hands. "By my powers as Queen of the Dark Realm, I bind thee, human child called Peter. You may speak no answer should the mortal world come in search of you— your form shall be cloaked, your true self hidden. The Dark Court surrounds you, and here you shall bide."

As she spoke, thin streams of blackish light came from her hands and wrapped around him like cold spiderwebs. Bug shivered.

"I don't like it," he said. "I don't wanna bide here." Whatever *bide* even meant, anyway.

"You have no choice." The Queen smiled at him, hard and cruel, and closed her hands into fists.

The light faded, but he could still feel the patterns laid against his skin.

"Puck?" He turned, to see that the faerie had retreated almost to the edge of the clearing. "Can we go back now?"

"Alas. I must leave you here, youngling." Puck tipped his head, the twinkle in his eyes extinguished. "It is the will of the Realm."

Fear rose up in Bug, thick and choking in his throat. He didn't want to stay in this dark, creepy place!

"I want the adventure to be done," he said. "Please."

"This is just the beginning," Puck said. "Be brave."

Then the faerie whirled about three times in a flurry of leaves and stardust, and was gone.

Bug swallowed back a yell of protest, even though he wanted to throw himself on the ground, screaming and kicking. This was severely not fun.

"Pity we can't slice off his toes," said one of the sharp-toothed creatures. "Him looks tasty."

"Bruiseshank," the Queen said, her voice reprimanding, "obey the rules. No harm done unless it is visited upon his changeling first."

The creature spat into the moss. "Aye, your majesty."

The Dark Queen beckoned to a figure in the shadows. "Bard Thomas, take this boy away. I grow weary of his tiresome mortal presence."

"As my lady commands." A man stepped forward, with gray-brown hair and tired eyes. He had a guitar slung across his back, and was dressed in a blue tunic.

He was the most normal-looking guy in the whole creepy clearing, and Bug let out a breath of relief. At least the Queen wasn't going to feed him to the sharp-teeths.

"Hello." The man bent down when he got to Bug. "I am Thomas, and you are under my care for the time being. Will you come with me?"

Bug glanced around at the faeries. For sure he didn't want to stay there, the focus of gleaming eyes and spiderwebs made of weird light.

"Where are we going?" he asked.

"To my home," Thomas said. "It lies beyond the clearing."

"I'm hungry," Bug said, suddenly yearning for his abandoned breakfast. "Do you have any Sugar Crunchies cereal?"

The man blinked at him, a sudden half-smile warming his face. "Not precisely—but perhaps we shall find something that will suffice."

Bug wasn't sure he wanted to eat suff ice, whatever that was, but he shrugged.

"Okay," he said. "Let's go."

Thomas led him away from the flickering purple bonfire to a narrow pathway winding through the forest. Bug was glad to get out of the clearing, away from the mean faeries and the Queen's cold presence. At least this Thomas guy was more pleasant to be around.

Dark bushes with flat leaves grew on either side of the path, and the gnarled trees towered overhead, their branches making a noise like someone speaking in a different language. Maybe they were talking in *leaf* or *bark* or something.

Bug paused, listening. He felt like if he focused hard, he could understand what the trees were saying. Pretending his feet were roots and his arms were branches, he breathed slow and let the inside of his mind pay attention. Just as he was getting little bits of *itching bugs upon surface* and *air is wet*, Thomas circled back around and touched his shoulder.

"Are you well, youngling?" His old eyes were full of worry.

"I'm good. Just listening to the trees." Bug rubbed his face. He was too hungry to keep concentrating, anyway. Maybe later.

Thomas's brows rose, and he glanced up at the dark branches. "I suppose the breeze might whisper you stories. But come along—it's not far to my tent."

"You're *camping* here?" Bug glanced around. "Don't the

Queen and stuff have houses?"

"Some of them have dwelling places, above and below the ground—but I prefer my comforts, as you will see."

Bug didn't think a tent set up in the talking woods would be all that comfortable, but the camping part sounded fun. The few times he and Tam had camped out, he'd liked it.

The thought of his brother sent an anxious stab through his chest.

"Can I go home soon?" he asked. "I miss my family."

Thomas sighed. "I cannot say what will be, but your brother and his allies have their wits about them. Hopefully, your stay here will not be long."

Bug stuck his lips out in a frown, then glanced at the older man.

"What's a dard?" he asked.

"A dard?" Thomas blinked down at him.

"What the lady called you. Dard Thomas. Is that like a swear word here?"

"Ah." Thomas's lips twitched, like he was trying not to smile. "A Bard. It means a special kind of musician."

"And you're it?" That explained the guitar. "Can I hear you play? I love music."

"Certainly. Perhaps I even play some songs you know."

"Prime! I wanna hear *Crush It*. That's my favorite."

"Alas." Thomas held back a branch so that it didn't whip back and smack Bug in the head. "That song is not in my repertoire."

"That's okay. I'll teach it to you. Hey, what's that?"

Something glowed through the trees ahead, big and white like a huge lit-up marshmallow.

"That," Thomas said, "is my home."

CHAPTER 3

THE PATH MEANDERED a few more yards through the softly-speaking forest. As they got closer to Thomas's home, Bug saw that the glowing thing *was* a tent, but way bigger than what he'd imagined. It was tall enough that Thomas could stand up and probably even raise his arms over his head without touching the roof.

There was a real door, though it was made of the same material as the tent. Thomas held it open and gestured for Bug to go in.

He stepped inside, layers of colorful rugs cushioning his feet, and turned around in a circle, awe flashing through him. "Whoa—this is the most sparked tent ever. You even have different rooms in here!"

There was a kitchen with a small table and chairs, open shelves, and a counter on the left. On the right were a bunch of ploofy chairs and a long, low couch piled with cushions. Three curtained openings along the back wall showed glimpses of other rooms.

Bug never thought a tent in the forest could be bigger than his family's own *house*. It was crazy.

Thomas let the front door close, then walked across the living area to the doorway with a blue curtain drawn back on one side. "This is where you'll be staying."

Bug peeked in, to see a bed with a downy-looking comforter, more soft rugs, and a wooden shelf with things on it: a few black feathers, a sparkly rock, some old-school printed books with fancy covers.

"No sleeping bag," he said. It would be weird to wake up in an actual bed, instead of on the couch.

"Indeed." Thomas gave him a look, then went back into the main room. He took off his guitar, gently setting it on a carved wooden stand, then gestured to Bug. "Let us see if you like honey cakes as well as sugar cereal, shall we?"

"Sure." Bug's tummy felt hollow, and by that point he was happy to try anything. Even weird cakes. But honey sounded good.

He hopped onto one of the three chairs surrounding the table made of dark wood, then swung his heels back and forth and looked around the room some more.

Lanterns hung from the ceiling, but there wasn't fire inside, just round glows that moved around a little. They were speaking too, but so high-pitched he could barely hear them.

"Does everything here talk?" he asked Thomas.

The older man looked up from the counter, where he was setting golden rounds of cake onto a pottery plate.

"What do you mean?" he asked. Although his tone was mild, the look in his eyes was sharp.

Bug waved his arm. "The lights, the trees. Probably other

stuff, though I haven't heard it yet." Not his food though, he hoped.

"Curious," Thomas said quietly. "Have you encountered the faerie folk before this visit?"

"Well, yeah, I've seen Puck. And sometimes I have funny dreams at night."

"Fae-touched," Thomas murmured, setting the plate down on the table. "I should have expected it."

Bug wanted to ask what that meant, but he was distracted by the honey cakes in front of him. He picked one up, glad it wasn't too sticky, and took a big bite.

"Mm," he said around a mouthful of cake. "This is really good."

Thomas nodded at him. "Despite dwelling in the heart of the Dark Court, there is some pleasantness to be found."

"Do you have any milk?" Bug asked, needing something to wash his cake down with.

"Thistle milk is the closest thing to what you're used to in the mortal world. Would you like to try a mug?"

"Will it scratch my tongue?"

"No—though it's a bit tangy." Thomas waved his hand over an empty mug, muttering a few words in a singsong voice.

A moment later, the mug was half full of white liquid. He set it down in front of Bug.

"You can do magic?" Bug glanced into the cup, then back up at Thomas.

"Small summoning and transformations only. Nothing like the larger workings of faerie magic."

"Prime." Bug looked around the tent. If he squinted, he could tell that the rugs used to be leaves and moss, the chairs some kind of mushroom, the curtains bits of cobweb.

Thomas poured himself a mug of amber liquid from the teapot on the counter. Settling across from Bug, he selected a cake of his own.

"What're you drinking?" Bug asked.

"Blackberry tea. You're welcome to some, if you'd prefer."

Reminded of his thistle milk, Bug took a careful sip. The bard was right, it was kind of tangy—but not too bad. As long as you didn't expect it to taste like real milk.

"I must caution you." Thomas leaned forward. "While you are here, accept no food or drink unless it is from my hand. Otherwise, you might remain trapped forever in the Dark Court."

Bug shivered. "I wouldn't like that."

"No. You would not." Deep sorrow laced Thomas's voice.

Something in his tone made Bug glance at him suspiciously. "Wait. Are *you* trapped here forever? Did you eat something bad?"

"No." The man let out a heavy breath. "I freely chose to come, knowing I would never return to the mortal world."

"That doesn't sound okay. What if you wanted to go back, like, really a lot?"

"There is no point in such wishings. That door is closed to me—but others have opened in its place."

Something only an adult would say. Bug grabbed the last cake from the plate. "So would you play me a song?"

Maybe that would cheer Thomas up.

"Certainly." Thomas drained his mug of tea, then rose and got his guitar.

He pulled his chair out from the table a little more, then

sat down and plucked at the strings. A shimmery silver sound came from the instrument.

"That's way different from regular guitars, isn't it?" Bug asked. "Is it enchanted?"

Thomas gave him a small smile. "Indeed. Although my guitar resembles the one I owned in the mortal world, this one is made from the magic of the Realm of Faerie; crafted from a dryad's gift, inlaid with banshee's tears, and strung with starlight."

"Whoa." Bug tilted his head. "Yeah, I can see all that. It kinda glows."

"That it does." Thomas played another chord, then launched into a song that sounded familiar.

When he got to the chorus, Bug recognized it and joined in, his high voice blending in with the bard's strong tones.

"That's an old one," Bug said, when the song ended. He liked it, the words about believing and holding onto feelings. "Is it about magic?"

"Like all great pieces of music, it's about whatever you need it to be about."

"*Crush It* is the same. Like on different days, it means different stuff. Wanna learn it?"

"Certainly."

Bug hummed the short melody a couple times, beating the edge of the table with his fingers. Pretty soon, Thomas started picking out the notes on his guitar.

"It's not quite right, though," Bug said. "I mean, yeah, the song is right. But we need drums. Do you have drums?"

Thomas gave him a thoughtful look. "No—but I could create some. A hand drum, perhaps?"

"Oh, oh!" Bug scooted forward to the edge of his chair.

"Could you make me a drum kit? I've wanted one forever, but we don't have room and Tam always said they were too loud anyway." He glanced around Thomas's living room, then pointed at the corner by the couch. "I bet we could fit it over there. Especially if you took out some of the chairs."

"I suppose you are correct." A smile in his voice, Thomas stood. "We might repurpose the toadstools into a snare and toms."

"A rock for the kick drum?" Bug suggested, leaping to his feet. "What about cymbals? Dry leaves?"

"Yes. And the drumsticks will be easy enough to transform from holly sprigs." Thomas set his guitar back in the stand. "Very well, young Peter. We will gather a few more items from the forest, and construct you a drum kit beyond your wildest imagination."

"Prime!" Bug let out a cheer, then looked at Thomas. "That's not really my name, though. Not my real one."

"I know." The bard lowered his voice. "But it was well done of you to give it to the Queen, and so I shall call you thusly, that her leash be not so tight as she believes. Now, come. We have a drum kit to scavenge."

CHAPTER 4

CRUSH IT WAS way better with real drums, although it took a while for Bug to get the hang of how to play them. Sure, he'd played Drum Maniacs a ton, but using actual sticks on surfaces instead of waving game controllers around was severely different.

Thomas was patient, first tapping a beat on the body of his guitar for Bug to follow, then strumming chords. He even got them to mostly sound like the right ones for the song.

After a long while, Bug's arms got tired. He put the sticks down and looked at Thomas over the red and white drum kit surrounding him.

"Weird that it just stays dark here all the time," he said. "How do you know when it's time to sleep, or wake up?"

Thomas set his guitar aside, then stood up and stretched. "I tell time now by the moon and stars, and by the brush of the seasons as then pass overhead."

That didn't sound very precise. "But what about dinner?"

The bard smiled at him. "Are you suggesting you're hungry?"

"Well, yeah. Now that we've stopped."

While the honey cakes had been filling, that meal felt like a long time ago.

"Indeed." Thomas glanced up at the white canopy of the tent overhead. "It is past time to take a meal."

"What are we going to eat?" Bug hopped off the stool and went to join Thomas in the kitchen area. "Is it dinnertime in my world, too?"

Thomas pulled a loaf of bread off one shelf, and produced some cheese and apples from a cupboard that seemed magically refrigerated.

"Time does not move the same way in the Realm," he said, slicing a piece of bread. "It is likely that many dinner-times have been and gone in the mortal world. Perhaps more than usual, if Puck was successful in his attempts to intervene with the timeflow. An afternoon here could be a week or more in human time."

"Really?" Bug stared at him, worry scratching his heart. "But what about my mom? And Tam? Don't they miss me?"

"Steps have been taken to protect them both from the knowledge of your absence." Thomas gave him a look, then raised one eyebrow. "I suspect, however, that your brother is well aware of what has transpired, and is working diligently for your return."

Thomas brought their food to the table. Bug scooted into the chair across from the bard and grabbed some bread and cheese.

"Can I help him?" The question was somewhat muffled by the large bite of bread he'd just taken.

"There is little we can do but bide," Thomas said. "And

wish Tam and his allies all the luck in the Realm. I pray they arrive before the dark of the moon."

"When's that?"

"Tomorrow night." Thomas's voice was low, like he didn't want to say the words.

"And something bad's gonna happen?" The bread in Bug's mouth tasted dry, and he took a quick swallow from his refilled mug of thistle milk.

"If the Queen has her way, yes." Thomas frowned. "But it is wiser not to think of such things. There is still time. And we have a song to finish learning."

Bug understood. Sometimes there wasn't anything you could do about the bad stuff waiting in the future. Especially when you were just a kid. Besides, he was hungry. He picked up the last hunk of creamy white cheese and decided not to worry for a while.

"Do you have any friends who play bass?" he asked Thomas. "Or singers, too? That would be good on the *crush it* parts. The real song has a bunch of people singing there."

"An excellent plan." The sadness on Thomas's face lifted a little. "I will do my best to find the rest of our band. But now, finish your apple. It is time for you to go to bed."

"I'm not tired," Bug said, but even as he spoke the words, a great weariness crashed down over him.

He tried not to yawn, but Thomas saw him, and smiled.

"You'll find a washroom behind the middle curtain," the bard said. "When you're ready, I'll sing you a lullaby for pleasant dreams."

Bug wanted to say he wasn't a baby, but the idea of a soothing song actually sounded pretty good. It had been a pretty tweaked day, after all.

"Okay," he said. "And I'll think of a good name for our band."

True to Thomas's promise, Bug didn't have any bad dreams. He woke, a little confused at first, until he remembered that he was in Thomas's tent-house, in the Dark Court. The bed was way comfy, and he spent a few minutes just stretching out and wiggling his toes, enjoying the fact he wasn't cocooned in a slightly sweaty sleeping bag.

The air smelled spicy, and he could hear the clack of dishes as Thomas moved around in the kitchen.

I was gonna come up with a band name. He lay there for a while, thinking about possibilities, but couldn't settle on anything that seemed quite right. *Thomas and the Bug* sounded too much like some old group from the far-distant past. And *The Dark Court Rocks* wasn't quite right, either. If the queen didn't like their sound, she might end up making their name literal, and turn them all to stone or something. The thought made him turn uncomfortably under the blankets.

Once they got a few more people, or creatures, in the band, it would be easier to know what to call it. But for the moment, the grumbling in his stomach outweighed the warmth of the bed, and he got up.

The soft rugs scattered on the floor felt nice under his bare feet—not matted and sticky like at home. None of his family was much on the cleaning-up side.

"Good day," Thomas said, looking up with a smile as Bug

ambled into the kitchen area. "I hope you don't mind more honeycakes and fruit. I eat very simply here."

"That's fine." Bug yawned and ran a hand through his hair.

It was probably standing up, anyway. Tam was always trying to get him to brush it flat before he went to school, but even the times he could force the brush through the thick tangle, the effect never lasted more than an hour or two.

He settled at the table and began to eat the food Thomas set out.

"I couldn't think of the right name for our band," Bug said around a mouthful of honey cake. "We need more people. Or whatever."

"As to that," Thomas said, "I'm expecting a visitor or two who might be able to assist us on the musical front."

"Prime! What kind of visitor?" It was probably too much to hope for that there would be other kids in the Dark Court.

Thomas gave him a mysterious smile. "You'll have to wait and see."

"Okay." Bug licked his fingers clean, then hopped up from the table. "Can I practice the drums now?"

"Certainly." Thomas waved to the transformed furniture.

With a grin, Bug settled on the drummer's stool—literally a toadstool—and grabbed the sticks. He started bashing away, trying to coordinate his feet with his hands so that he could get the steady thud of the kick drum in time. An occasional cymbal bash to round things out, too, and a riff on the toms, yeah. It might not be on beat, exactly, but the drums made a glorious noise.

When he got back to his world, he'd totally have to figure out how to get a set of his own.

CHAPTER 5

JUST WHEN BUG was getting ready to stop bashing away on the drums for a bit, Thomas's first visitor arrived.

Although the creature who stepped through the flap door was about as tall as Bug, it wasn't another kid. In fact, it was definitely not human at all. It looked more like an angry hedgehog—if hedgehogs had long arms and spindly legs and orange eyes.

"Come in," Thomas said to his guest, nodding to a long tube strapped to the creature's back. "You brought your instrument, I see."

Huh, so this was the bass player? Bug cocked his head, wondering how the tube worked.

"Aye," the creature said in a rough, squeaky voice. He glanced around, his fierce gaze falling on Bug. "Be this the mortal child?"

"Yes." Thomas gestured for Bug to come closer. "Furze, this is Bug."

Some of the heat went out of the creature's eyes. "Bug? A proper name for the Dark Realm."

"Um, thanks?" Bug didn't know if that was a compliment or not. He pointed to the instrument on Furze's back. "What is that, and how do you play it?"

The creature gave him a toothy grin. "My *artawirr*, it is."

Furze slung it off his back and brought one end of the tube to his mouth. Bug wasn't sure if he was blowing into it or humming or what, but a low, thrumming noise issued from the other end. It was like a bass, but even deeper, tickling the soles of Bug's feet and seeming to vibrate the whole tent.

"Prime!" Bug glanced at Thomas. "Can it match your chords though?"

Furze lifted his head and the noise stopped. "Do ye take me for an untutored thistlebrush? Of course I can."

Bug went up on his toes. "Let's try it."

"Wait a moment more," Thomas said, a smile in his voice. "The others will be here soon, and it's generally polite to offer refreshments to guests before putting them to work."

"Okay." Bug subsided, but he couldn't help the excitement sparking through him. He'd always wanted to be in a band. Whoever thought that being kidnapped by the faeries would make one of his most cherished dreams come true?

Though he did miss Tam and his mom, with a distant ache—like banging his arm on the edge of the counter and knowing it would leave a bruise that lasted for days. It wasn't too painful yet, though.

Furze laid his whirr-whatever down near the drum set, and Thomas went to the door of his tent again. He pulled it open to allow three faerie maidens to enter in a swirl of gossamer wings and silvery light.

Bug squinted. They were very pretty, in a strange, elongated way. He thought maybe he recognized the purple-winged one from the Dark Court. She'd stood right behind the queen's throne, and the memory of that meeting made him shiver a tiny bit.

"Thistledown, Briar, Yarrow, this is Bug," Thomas said, escorting the faeries to where Bug stood.

"Hi," Bug said with a little wave. "So you guys sing?"

They laughed with a sound like wind chimes, and purple-wing—Thistledown—leaned over him.

"Indeed," she murmured. "We sing to mortals in their sleep, and they wake haunted and grieving."

Bug glanced at Thomas. The chorus of *Crush It* wasn't exactly slow and sad.

"Fret not," the bard said. "These maidens also sing the Faerie Rade into battle." He frowned and turned to busy himself in his kitchen.

"A raid?" Bug asked Thistledown. "Like, endgame stuff?"

The faerie blinked at him, her big eyes confused. At least, he thought the misty look on her face was confusion.

"Nay," Furze said. "We ride out in procession. That is the Faerie Rade."

"Oh."

One of the other girls nodded, her hair shimmering like starlight on a puddle. "This very night, to Miles Cross we ride. To make the sacrifice—"

"Tea is ready," Thomas said abruptly, stepping forward with two steaming mugs.

He handed one to Furze and one to Bug, then gave the maidens little delicate glasses of some cloudy liquid. They all moved over to the table, where plates of honey cakes and fruit awaited.

Bug didn't think he'd get tired of honey cakes. Ever. They were even better than Sugar Crunchies.

The faerie girls didn't say much as they ate and sipped, but Furze and Thomas kept the conversation going. As they finished up, Thomas had Bug teach everybody the words of the chorus, and then the melody. The third time Bug sang it through, the maidens joined him, their voices clear and sweet and full of harmonies that made his breath catch.

"That's perfect," he said. "This is gonna rock."

"Let us add the instruments." Thomas nodded to the corner.

"Yeah!" Bug jumped up and raced over to the drum set.

He got settled, Thomas slung on his guitar, and Furze picked up his tube. The maidens ranged themselves by Thomas, their big eyes widening when Bug started pounding out the beat.

The first couple times through the song were... well, not that prime. Furze wasn't picking up all the changes, and half the time the faerie girls didn't know when to start singing—or when to stop.

Thomas called a break, then worked with Furze on getting the low tones right. Bug slipped off the stool and stretched his arms, which were feeling kinda sore from all the drumming he'd been doing. The maidens watched him as though he were some weird creature not of their world. Which, he supposed, was true.

"Tell me more about this Faerie Rade thing," he said to Thistledown.

She glanced at the other maidens, then turned to him. "The entire Court mounts upon their steeds—or goes by foot or cart or wing—and traverses the countryside. It is a grand sight indeed, to see the Queen and her Black Knight and all the members of the Dark Realm arrayed in their finery."

"You dress up?" Bug thought they looked fancy as it was, with their pale flowy dresses and sparkles in their hair.

Thistledown nodded.

"And sometimes you fight stuff? Furze said you sing in your battles."

"Aye," the faerie said softly.

It sounded interesting. Better than hanging around in Thomas's tent, waiting for stuff to happen. "Are you fighting in this next one? Do I get to come?"

"That is our Queen's intent." There was a sorrowful note in her voice.

Thomas glanced up sharply, his eyes narrowing.

"Come," he said. "I think Furze is ready. And when it's time to sing, I will nod my head at you, Thistledown. Until then, silence is the best course."

She moved away from Bug, and he hopped back behind the drums.

This time, the song actually sounded a lot more like the version of *Crush It* in Bug's head.

"Yeah!" he said when they got to the end. "Let's do it again."

"I pray thee, do not," came a dry voice from the doorway.

Bug glanced up, to see a big black cat sauntering into the tent. A talking cat, obviously.

"Greetings, milord Dubh," Thomas said, putting his hands flat on his guitar and making the creature a slight bow. "What brings you to visit?"

The cat sat and wrapped his tail over his front paws. He

had a white spot on his chest, and a thin gold circlet on his head, like he was a king or something.

"The Court commands you cease this—if I might put it indelicately—caterwauling racket," he said. "It is disturbing to the sensibilities of all nearby."

A smile crept over Thomas's lips. "Is it, indeed? Alas, please inform the Court that, as Queen's Bard, it is necessary for me to practice my art."

"Oh ho?" The cat's yellow gaze moved to Bug. "Before now, your music was much more pleasing to the ear, bard."

"All things change," Thomas said. "Even in the Realm. Convey my regrets to the Queen that I cannot obey her command at this time."

The cat sniffed and got to his feet, tail lashing. "I suppose this will end soon enough, as you well know. Have your fun while you may."

Feline head held high, he stalked out of the tent. The faerie maidens looked at each other, wings fluttering with what Bug thought was nerves, although Furze didn't seem particularly bothered by the big cat's visit.

"Shall we play it again?" Thomas asked, raising his brows at Bug.

"You won't get in trouble?"

The bard shrugged. "There is trouble, and then there is Trouble. I might earn the Queen's mild displeasure, but not her wrath. Now, count us in."

"Okay." Bug raised his drumsticks, gave them four beats, and off they went once more into the satisfying clamor of *Crush It.*

CHAPTER 6

REHEARSAL ENDED A LITTLE LATER, and Bug was actually kind of glad because his arms were feeling like noodles by then.

"Can we play again tomorrow?" he asked as Thomas ushered his guests to the door.

Furze grunted a goodbye and left, but Thistledown turned and put her cool, delicate fingers to Bug's cheek. Her touch was like a soft, cold wind, there and then gone again before he could blink.

"This has been an unexpected pleasure, young mortal," she said. "Stay strong and true."

"Um, okay." He glanced into her wide and shining eyes. "I liked meeting you. You guys sing really well."

She gave him a sad smile, a nod, and then left. Once the tent was empty except for the two of them, Thomas set his hand on Bug's shoulder. It was warm and human, and comforting. A wave of homesickness rushed through Bug, and he blinked back the wetness in his eyes.

"Can I go home yet?" he asked.

Thomas let out a heavy sigh. "If all goes well, perhaps

there is a chance. Come to the table—I must speak with you about what is to come."

Anxiety shivered through Bug. He sat, swinging his heels and trying not to feel like a scared little kid. "What's going on?"

Moving stiffly, Thomas took the chair across from him.

"As Thistledown said, the Faerie Rade is quickly approaching—and we are to join it." Thomas held up his hand, stopping Bug's questions. "There are some... events planned which will be frightening to you."

"Like what?" Bug didn't like the sound of it one bit.

Thomas rubbed his forehead. "My binding to the Dark Court prevents me from saying. Just know that, no matter the peril, there is always hope."

"Can't I just go home?" Bug's voice sounded thin in his ears.

"If only it were that simple. But we are expected at Court in a few hours—and I recommend you try and get some rest."

The last thing he felt was tired, especially after Thomas's mysterious hints that something bad was going to happen.

"Do I have to?" he asked—meaning everything.

"I will make you a soothing draught." Thomas rose and put the kettle on. "It will help you sleep. And make the strangeness of the Rade easier to bear. The sight of the Wild Hunt alone is enough to drive most mortals into a panic. Although, of anyone, you might be able to gaze openly upon them."

"I just want Tam." Bug set his chin on his fists and stared blankly as Thomas sifted herbs into the teapot.

"As do I, my friend. As do I."

Whatever it was Thomas gave him to drink, it did help the whirl of Bug's thoughts quiet down. To his surprise, he slept, waking groggy and a little numb when Thomas shook his shoulder.

"Arise," the bard said. "It is time."

"Okay," Bug mumbled, trying to wake up. He felt wrapped in fog—but cozy pink fog, more like cotton candy than something wet and gray.

Time seemed to speed up, then slow down, because what felt like a second later they stood on the mossy ground in front of the Dark Queen's throne. Pale purple light illuminated the clearing, showing the gathered fey folk. Some wore feathers, some bones. Some were elegantly winged, others squat and vicious—but all of them glittered somehow, like broken glass in the moonlight.

"Have you ensured the boy will remain biddable?" the queen asked in her sharp, dangerous voice.

"I have," Thomas said, sounding unhappy.

She gave him a long, considering look, then turned her icy gaze on Bug. "Nonetheless, I shall renew the spell to bind his tongue from speech. In dealings with these particular mortals it is best to be entirely sure."

Thomas bowed, his expression strained. "As you wish, my lady."

She raised her hands, dark light flickering between her fingers, then pointed at Bug. A strange tingling sensation filled his mouth, like he'd bitten on a wasp and it had stung his tongue.

"Ow," he tried to say, but when he opened his mouth, no sound came out.

"Good." The queen smiled. It was not a nice-looking smile. "Bard Thomas, take your place in the Rade. I shall conceal the mortal within the ranks of my court. Just in case something untoward should occur."

Thomas gave Bug's shoulder a squeeze. "Don't give up," he said, so quietly that Bug barely heard him.

Then he was gone, and the cackles and cries of the Dark Court swept over Bug like a cold wind.

He blinked, and was surrounded by faerie maidens in their shining silky dresses. Thistledown stood near him, her pale purple wings moving as slowly as a heartbeat. The sky flashed, dark and light and dark again.

He blinked again, and found he was being carried in a sling-type thing, with half a dozen of the maids on either side, bearing him up. Above their heads, he could just glimpse the form of the Dark Queen astride a horse. She wore a black cloak that glittered like the night sky and swirled in the wind. A glowing figure rode beside her, so bright that Bug had to squint, like he was looking into the sun.

All around him was the sound of unearthly creatures chittering, clacking, chiming. To cover up the strangeness, he started humming *Crush It* as loud as he could. At least he could still sing.

They were moving down a road, but the landscape around them was weird and woozy—the brush-covered hillsides bucking up and down like they were alive, the sky overhead streaked with neon colors like out of some crazy vid.

Then the procession stopped. Up ahead Bug could see tall

stones sticking up into the air and glowing with a soft silver light. The faerie girls set him down and he got groggily to his feet, but he still couldn't go anywhere. They hemmed him in, a fence of pale and shimmering maidens.

He could hear the queen speaking, and other voices that sounded... human. And familiar. One of them was his brother's, he was sure of it.

"Tam!" he tried to yell, but only silent air came out of his open mouth.

Frustrated tears leaked from the corners of his eyes, and he shoved at the faerie girls, but they didn't budge. For such delicate creatures, they were as impossible to move as a circle of streetlights set into concrete.

But then Tam started singing, and Bug sagged with relief as the words of *Crush It* floated to him from somewhere up ahead. It was his brother first, and then a couple girl's voices joined in. He pulled in a big breath and when they got to the chorus, he sang it as loud as he could.

"*Oh baby then we crush it,*" he belted out.

Thistledown was the first to step away, and her friends followed her, until Bug stood in an empty patch of the road. Then Tam was there, in front of him, hope and fear stark in his eyes.

"Bug, are you okay?" he asked in a strained voice.

"Hi Tam." Bug tried to run forward, but his feet were stuck like glue. "Can we go home now?"

"That's the plan." His brother gave him a crooked smile.

"Alas." The dark queen nudged her scary-looking horse forward. "We have other plans for you, mortals."

She gestured to the Faerie Rade behind her, and the rattle of weapons was loud in the stillness.

"Attack!" the shining guy beside her cried.

With loud, guttural cries, the creatures of the Dark Court surged past.

"Take cover," Tam yelled at Bug as the Black Knight raised his sword.

Bug turned, and was swept up in strong, human arms. Thomas.

"Let me go." He squirmed, trying to get away. "I have to get to Tam!"

"Bide, child," Thomas said, grunting as he attempted to hold on to Bug. "You would only endanger yourself. Thistledown, your assistance if you please."

The faerie maid swooped over and laid one finger on Bug's forehead. All around them was the sound of fighting. He struggled and thrashed. Tam. He had to get to Tam.

"Hush," Thistledown said in her soft voice.

Coldness pierced his head, like the worst ice-cream headache ever, and then the world went dark.

CHAPTER 7

BUG WOKE in a confusion of terror and bright flashes of light. Above him, red and blue fire danced, illuminating the terrifying faces of the Dark Queen and the bright guy, who also wore a crown. Cords bound Bug's body, and he lay on something cold and hard. He couldn't move his head enough to see if Tam was there—or anyone else who could help him.

Despite himself, he let out a little whimper.

Then everything happened at once, like some disjointed nightmare. Tam and his girlfriend Jennet knelt at his side, and they were going to save him... and then they were snatched back, but Marny's uncle Zeg yelled really loud, broke the bindings holding Bug down, and scooped him up in his arms.

A scary guy Bug remembered from the queen's court, with dark antlers on his head, pushed Zeg back to the flat rock. Then the bright king grabbed Bug away, his fingers digging in like talons. The earth spun and tilted.

Blades flashed, and Jennet sang a high, clear note, There was a feeling like lightning had just flashed down among the standing stones, sizzling and stunning everyone into temporary stillness.

In that moment, Tam was there, demanding the king release them. The grasp on Bug's shoulder loosened, and with a wrench, Bug was free.

"Tam, Tam." He threw himself at his brother.

"I'm here." Carefully, his sword in his other hand, Tam gave him a tight hug.

The tall stones around them burst into purple flames. The air turned cold, and a sound like low thunder boomed over the hills.

And then the dragon came.

It was huge, and black, and hovered right over the circle of stones. Behind it Bug could see other dragons circling overhead, in every color he could imagine, and some he'd never thought of. The faerie folk huddled and shivered away —all except for the two standing in the center.

The dragon spoke; at least Bug thought it spoke, though not in any language he could remember ever hearing. Still, though he didn't catch the words, he could tell the faeries were in big, big trouble.

Tam backed away, bringing Bug with him, and went over to where Jennet lay on the ground. She looked really bad, her arm bleeding from a long slice, a thin silver sword in her other hand.

An adult wearing orange robes rushed to her side and started helping Tam bind up Jennet's wound. Another guy Bug recognized as going to Tam's school staggered over. Meanwhile, the black dragon hung overhead and the air trembled.

It was all confused, and Bug rubbed his eyes, trying to

make sense of events. Was this the end? The beginning? Why were they still in the faerie lands?

Puck dashed up, riding on a red fox, and speaking in riddles.

"She is here," the sprite said.

"We don't have time for your jokes, Puck," Tam said, though Bug didn't see that it was funny in any way.

The other boy stared at Puck, then scooped the fox up in his arms. With an annoyed yelp, Puck jumped off. He floated gently to the ground, then turned to Bug.

"I know all this is rich and strange, mortal child," he said. "And I am sorry."

He reached out his long, crooked fingers and put his hand on Bug's chest. The touch tingled, but it didn't hurt, and Bug wasn't too scared. Not like when the other faeries had him.

"What are you doing?" he asked.

"Speeding time for you," the sprite replied. "Too long in the presence of the Twilight Kingdom's magic is not salubrious for one of your years."

Whatever that meant. Bug shrugged his shoulders.

"Close your eyes, and count to three," Puck said.

Bug did. Well, almost. He kept his eyelids slitted to see what was going on—and to make sure he didn't lose Tam. After the count of two, he was sorry, though. Tam was still there, but everything was moving in a super-fast blur that made him feel dizzy and sick.

"Three," he said, finally closing his eyes all the way.

The prickling feel of Puck's touch faded, and Bug's ears popped, like he'd just gone down a hill really fast on his gravboard.

"Look about you," the sprite said. "You have but a few

more moments in the Realm before I send you back to the mortal world."

"That's okay. I'm ready to go." Bug blew out a breath, then turned in a circle, worry spiraling through him. "Where's Tam?"

His brother was gone. And so was almost everyone else, except Jennet—who looked a lot better than before he'd closed his eyes—and the orange-robed guy who was talking to Thomas. Even the dragons had left, and of the faerie folk there were only a few stragglers left, scattered around the stones. At least the creepy king and queen were gone.

"Your brother has already returned to his place," Puck said.

Bug walked a little unsteadily over to Jennet.

"I wanna go home," he said, suddenly feeling like he was a little kid again, not a brave adventurer or a rock star.

Jennet put her arm around his shoulders and he leaned into her warm, human touch.

"Me too," she said, sounding really tired. "Puck, help us out?"

"Fear not." The sprite grinned, then leaned over and whispered something in Jennet's ear.

"I will," she said, giving Bug a squeeze.

"Then I bid you farewell." Puck did a handspring, his tattered tunic ruffling in the breeze. He straightened up and winked at Bug. "Til we meet again."

Golden light whirled out of nowhere, and Bug could hear Puck laughing, high and merry, as the Realm of Faerie dissolved around him.

∾

The first thing Bug saw was a fancy tan-colored living room. The second thing he saw was his mother.

"Mom!" he cried, dashing over to where she stood beside a big window.

He jumped and she bent, arms wide open to catch him.

"My boy." Her voice was soft and full of love, and Bug tried to ignore the strange faraway look in her eyes.

"Hey, it's the Bug," a voice said.

He glanced over to see Tam's friend Marny sitting on one of the couches. She had a smudge on one cheek and her hair was a wild frizz, but she looked way happy to see him.

"I saw your uncle," he said.

"Good." She nodded. "Was everybody all right? After... whatever happened?"

"I think so. Jennet wasn't sad or anything. Hey, where is she?" He wiggled, and his mom put him down.

"Not here," Marny said. "But hopefully the gang will be back soon. Since it looks like they won."

"Won what? And where is here?"

"Won you," Marny said simply. "And we're at Spark's place. Hey, there's some leftover pizza. You hungry?"

"Starvelating."

Marny set him up at a low table with pizza, soda, and once he was pretty much full, an orange popsicle. It was the best meal he'd ever had. Even better than honey cakes.

"Miss Jaxley is arriving," a metallic-sounding voice announced from somewhere near the ceiling.

He glanced up. "Who was that?"

"The house." Marny looked at him and shook her head. "Wipe your face, then we can go meet them."

His mom swabbed at him with paper napkins, thankfully,

for once, not licking them to get the worst of the stickiness off him, and then Marny led them out of the room. Outside stretched a long hallway lit with soft golden light, and he blinked at how sparkly everything was. The floor was made of shiny stone and the air smelled like rich people.

Then the front door opened. Bug caught a glimpse of the night outside as a bunch of people came in—but the only who mattered was his brother. Was Tam there, really, or was it all a big trick?

"Bug?" Tam called, his voice uncertain.

"Tam!" Bug cried, pelting forward, his heart hot in his chest.

Then he was wrapped in his big brother's embrace, clasped against Tam's rough jacket and snuffling back tears. His pulse beat wildly with joy and relief, and his legs felt like noodles, barely able to hold him up.

A moment later, he felt their mom come up and put her arms around them both, holding on fast, and just like that he was back where he belonged. He was home.

REAL CHALLENGE

THE GIANT WOULD HAVE BEEN SILLY, if he wasn't so terrifying.

A tiny green hat perched jauntily on his sparsely-haired head, his pasty skin glowing pale beneath. His red eyes bulged over a crooked nose and cracked-tooth grimace. And his wickedly sharp axe was stained with blood. Some developer had made sure to take every kid's nursery rhyme and turn it into nightmare.

When she'd started playing *Giant Killer*, Spark Jaxley had expected something fluffier. Now she was stuck in solo mode and facing up against the final boss—this giant who'd already smashed her character into a pulp two times now.

She should have read the 'dits on the brand new game before diving in—but it was too late now. Who knew the developers would make a solo win basically impossible? Not every gamer could party up with friends, after all.

"Grind your bones," the giant said, the rumble of his voice shaking the tabletop. "I smell you, little human."

Spark adjusted her grip on her glowing blue sword and peered around the salt shaker she was using for cover. The grains were the size of rocks, the transparent shaker twice as high as her head. Being teeny-tiny was a serious disadvantage, but one that every player in this fight had to deal with, solo or not.

She'd specced her character all wrong for this encounter, though. Sword Mage was a great damage-doing class, but she should have built a tank. DPS and speed had, so far, not been a match for the giant's fists and axe.

Time to smarten up. She'd been arrogant, and it had made her dumb. Sure, she was the best rated single-play gamer in the country, but she hadn't won the national title by making stupid mistakes over and over.

"Fee Fie," the giant said, which was the signal for his first enrage.

The first time Spark had died, it'd been to an enormous fist crushing down on her. At least she'd figured out how to avoid that attack.

"Yoo-hoo," she said, stepping out from behind the salt and waggling her sword at the giant. "Over here."

Her monstrous opponent growled and lifted his fists. There was almost time for Spark to get a magebolt off at the giant's face. Almost, but not quite...

"Argh!" the giant yelled, his hands crashing down like twin meat hammers.

At the last second, Spark darted away. Her heart hammering in her throat, she fetched up against the pepper. One mega-attack survived. Two to go.

The giant lifted his fists and inspected them for the smear of dead human, giving Spark a few moments to set her hotkeys and plan her next move. In order to activate her biggest spell, she'd need to trigger an area-of-effect first. Ideally, where it would do the most damage.

She glanced up at her foe, judging the distance to his face. Surely his eyes were vulnerable. Unfortunately, they were also out of range.

Okay then, something closer. Last time she'd targeted his hands, but he'd just pulled out his axe and cleaved her in half. Not pretty.

However, there was one area that was in reach. And hopefully a good target for her Arcane Burn spell.

She sidled around the glass-sided pepper shaker and eyed the distance to the edge of the table. The giant's metal belt buckle scraped up against the wood, so she'd have to veer off slightly to cast her spell.

Groin shot—that was the plan. Spark dashed into the open, sword raised.

The giant let out a cackle. "Bake my bread."

"I'll bake *your* bread," Spark said under her breath, dodging back and forth to avoid the giant's blows.

She scooted to the edge of the vast table. Pointing the tip of her blade at the area below the giant's belt, she ignited her Arcane Burn.

Please, do some damage.

"Foe," the giant growled.

The word vibrated through Spark's chest. In the corner of her vision, the sim interface flickered, showing her biggest spell was charging up. Quarter power. Then halfway there. Why wasn't that Arcane Burn doing damage?

Crack!

Splinters of wood flew from the axe blow that had

narrowly missed her head. She rolled to her feet and glanced up at her red-faced foe. No more distractions.

With a deep breath, she charged forward, straight at the giant's belly. The axe swished through the air behind her, the blade embedding into the table.

Good.

While the giant wrenched it out, she leaped. For one heart-stopping second she was airborne over a huge drop. The giant's leather shoes seemed a thousand feet below, and she knew the fall would kill her.

Then she managed to catch herself one-handed on the edge of the leather belt. Gasping, she drove her blade into the giant's hip.

With a howl of pain, her opponent doubled over—bringing his face into range.

Her Kill Bolt reached maximum, and without a second's hesitation, she triggered the spell, aiming at the giant's near eye.

Direct hit.

Finally, her luck was holding.

"Fum!" the giant cried, staggering upright.

Gritting her teeth, Spark held on to his belt as he lurched back and forth. She slammed against the buckle and grimaced. But she had to stay alive until the giant went down for good.

Otherwise, she'd respawn at the bottom of a giant vine reaching up into the clouds, and she didn't have time to play this whole encounter again.

Especially as her parents refused to let her miss dinner when she was gaming. One time, they'd even sent her older brother into her room to physically pull the plug on her sim-chair. Not only had she been nauseous the rest of the night, she'd never forgiven him.

But she'd never missed dinner again.

Dammit, though, was this giant ever going to die?

He stumbled toward the table again, and Spark judged the distance. Too far to jump.

"Sparkie!" It was her younger sister's voice, filtering through the helmet. "Mom says come eat."

"Sec," she ground out, not sure if Rosie could hear her.

Die, already.

Finally, the giant stiffened and started toppling over. Spark rode him to the ground, jumping clear at the last second onto the ragged mat covering the wide plank floor of the giant's kitchen.

Her opponent let out a last moan, and the interface showing his vitality winked to black.

Victory! The word blinked across her visor. *Play Again?*

Spark lifted her finger, toggling the *No*.

"Mom says now, or else," Rosie said, tapping Spark's shoulder.

"Yeah. I know." Spark scrolled through the standings. There—top of the solo plays. *Spark Jaxley.*

Grinning, she lifted her helmet. Untangling a lock of her magenta hair from the visor, she set it aside, then stripped off her gaming gloves.

"Did you win?" Rosie asked, squinting at the sim equip.

"Yes. Barely." Spark slid out of the chair. "Smells like potatoes."

Her little sister nodded. "I'm tired of them."

Spark was, too, but she gave her sister an encouraging

smile. "You know Mom and Dad are saving to send Jake to university this fall."

"But we'll have to eat potatoes for *years*," Rosie said. "You want to go to college too, and then me."

"Don't worry." Spark squeezed her little sister's shoulders. "I've got a plan."

Whether or not she could talk her parents into it, though...

They didn't understand about her gaming. Didn't realize that the money could be more than the handful of small sponsorships she'd picked up in the last year.

Winning the national title was big. But the World Gaming Championships were coming up in two months. The prize money alone was significant, but Spark had her sights set on something bigger.

VirtuMax, the top sim-gaming company in the world, had announced it was going to select a winner from the international competition to become their representative gaming star. Rumors were that they were developing a top-secret gaming system, better than any sim equipment built to-date, with an amazing interface and fantastic new immersive content to go with it.

Spark was determined to win the tournament's solo category. And even more set on scooping up the VirtuMax sponsorship.

She just had to talk her parents into letting her compete, which was going to be the toughest part of all.

~

"No," her dad said, passing the potatoes to Mom. "We can't afford to send you to Japan for some gaming thing."

"But Dad—"

"Shut it," Jake said, frowning at Spark. "I can't believe you're even asking them to do this. You know it's hard enough saving up for uni for me."

Inwardly, Spark seethed at her brother. If only her family could see what a great chance this was.

"It's during break, so I won't miss any school. And the gaming club said they'd help with finances."

"We don't need handouts," her mom said, spooning some mashed potatoes onto Nana's plate. "We're managing now, as long as we don't try to plan extravagant trips around the world."

Managing—barely. Spark glanced around the table. Three kids, her parents, plus Nana and Papa, all surviving on Dad's paycheck. Things had been easier when Mom still worked, but then Spark's elderly grandparents had needed to move in with them, and Mom became their full-time caregiver.

Not that Spark resented Nana and Papa. Family was important... which was why she had to get to Tokyo for the international competition. It was the best thing she could do to take care of her family.

"Let's say you win this thing," Dad said, glancing at her. "Then what?"

"If I can get the VirtuMax sponsorship, it's worth a lot of money," she said. "Enough to get Jake through university, plus save some for when it's my turn, and Rosie's. Then you guys could hire someone to help, and Mom could have more time."

"You're not dropping out of high school to play sim games," her mom said, her tone stern. "That's not a viable career path. You know we want better for you kids than what we had."

"But Mom, gaming is a real thing," Rosie piped up.

Spark glanced gratefully at her sister. At least somebody understood.

"Eat your potatoes," their mother said. "We're done talking about this."

"Well, now," Papa said in his slow, calm voice. "Maybe Sparkie has a point. Maybe she can do this."

"I can," Spark said. "I promise. And VirtuMax provides tutors and stuff. It wouldn't be like dropping out. I'd still get an education."

"Enough." Her dad set down his fork and gave her a pointed look. "Right now, our focus is on Jake. Maybe next year you can do the world tournament."

Next year would be too late. VirtuMax would have picked their sim star.

But Spark kept her mouth shut. Arguing any more would just make her parents more set against her going.

She let the dinner conversation wash around her: Jake's plans for on-campus housing, Rosie's current vid obsession, Papa's slow commentary on the weather. Nana didn't talk, but then, she was generally in some other world. Usually the past.

Dad didn't say much, either. He'd been working long hours and, glancing at the tired lines around his eyes, Spark wanted to apologize for asking for them to send her to the tournament. If only they understood how much her winning would mean—for all of them.

"Help me back to my chair, Sparkie," Papa said when they'd finished eating. "The dishes can wait."

Mom was already off with Nana, tucking her into bed, and Dad didn't seem to care if the table got cleared right away.

"Of course." Spark helped her grandfather stand, then carefully guided him to the overstuffed recliner where he spent much of his time.

He sat, somewhat shakily, and kept hold of her hand.

"Listen," he said in a low voice. "I want you to take my silver dollar collection. Use it to get to that game competition you want to attend."

A lump rose in Spark's throat. "I can't do that."

He patted her hand. "I insist. There's a rare Morgan in there that should sell for plenty."

"But you need that money."

He smiled at her. "You can pay me back. I believe in you, honey. Now, I keep that collection under the mattress. Soon as your mom leaves the bedroom, I want you to go in and get it."

"I..." Spark blinked back tears. She shouldn't do it. Her family was barely making ends meet. If Papa sold that coin for the family, instead, it was guaranteed money.

"Promise me," Papa said. "Go and win that competition. Tell your parents your school had a donor who gave you the funds. All right?"

She swallowed and concentrated on staying calm. Bursting into tears would be a dead giveaway to the rest of the family.

She drew in a shaky breath. "Okay. I love you, Papa."

"I love you, too." He squeezed her hand, then closed his eyes. "I'll be cheering for you."

This one's for you, Papa.

Spark flicked her fingers, the gaming gloves turning the movement into a half dozen torpedoes zinging out from her spacecraft. They locked onto her target, the enemy ship *Assassin*, and began exploding against the shields.

The watching crowd of several thousand people let out a cheer, the sound like the roar of waves, and she knew that millions more were viewing the gaming championships livestream.

Her grandpa was cheering her on, too—but not from this world. Not any more.

Two weeks before she was due to leave for Tokyo, he'd fallen in the kitchen. She and her siblings had been at school, and Mom was bathing Nana. By the time her mom found Papa, he'd slipped into unconsciousness.

Three days later, he was gone.

In the stunned aftermath, nobody challenged Spark's announcement that she was going to the tournament. Although she'd winced at the lie, it was true that there had been a donor. Just not an anonymous one through the school. Dad had agreed to let her go, since the money was there, and Mom had signed the paperwork in a fog. Maybe trying to make amends to Papa.

"It's not your fault," Spark had said, giving her mom a hug. "You and Dad both know that having Nana and Papa here was the best thing for them. For all of us." No matter how financially difficult, it was still a lot cheaper than a nursing home, and they'd gotten way better care.

"He would have wanted to go like that," Jake said. "You know he didn't want to fade away."

Mom had scrubbed the tears from her face and nodded, but Spark suspected it would take a long time for the shadow of guilt in her eyes to fade.

Spark's grief over Papa tangled up with insane excitement that she was actually signed up for the World Championships—ticket bought, hotel booked. When she'd stepped out of the plane in Narita Airport, she'd been thrilled to see fans waiting, wearing magenta wigs to show their allegiance.

"Spark!" they'd screamed. "Spark Jaxley!"

Despite the mix of emotions spiraling through her, she'd blasted through the prelims. Now it was down to her, the Korean world champion Jae-jin, a girl from Norway named Asa, and a surprisingly skilled contender from South Africa, Enzokuhle.

But Enzo wouldn't be in the competition much longer, if Spark had any say in the matter. His ship, the *Assassin*, was going down.

Enzo's ship returned fire, but she was already twisting away, using the gravity well of a nearby collapsing star to pull her own craft out of range. She planned to slingshot around and come at him point blank, lasers firing.

It was a move that would either wipe her out of the competition entirely, or advance her to the final round. But then, taking calculated risks was the essence of gaming. Balancing on the edge of challenge and skill, pushing your limits, and then, having stacked the odds in your favor as much as possible, rolling the dice.

"Come *on*," she murmured under her breath as the control panel of her ship started to flash red.

Too much stress, too much torque.

The stars blurred in her vision as the insane pull of the gravity well warped space around her ship. It was all she could do to keep the controller pointed forward. Sweat prickled the back of her neck, stung her eyes.

The interface began to shake. Sirens sounded, echoing through her head. From someplace far away, she heard the crowd yelling. For her, against her, it didn't matter.

Warning. Implosion in three seconds. The alert flashed across her visor.

Almost. There.

Two seconds.

The claxons drowned out everything except her heartbeat. She kept her eyes, and ship, pointed ahead, to a single bright point of light floating beyond the well.

One.

Her ship burst free, almost on top of the *Assassin*, and Spark clenched her hands, activating her laser array. A brilliant, deadly rain shot out, covering her enemy.

"No way!" Enzo shouted. "Dammit, Jaxley."

He twisted, trying to maneuver his ship out of the way, but it was too late.

Laughing, Spark flipped her craft over as she shot past, keeping the *Assassin* under heavy fire. She was upside down, her own ship shaking to bits, but Enzo went down first.

A beautiful blossom of light exploded across her visor. The *Assassin* was gone.

WINNER flashed in green letters across her vision. *Round complete.*

Somewhere, she hoped Papa was smiling.

She lifted her helmet to the deafening cheers of the crowd. More and more people sported pink hair now, even the guys. She dabbed the sweat out of her eyes, then got out of her sim chair and waved. The noise got even louder.

Across from her, Enzo stepped out of his rig.

"Good game," he said, extending his hand.

"You too." She gave him a firm handshake. "I mean it— you're a prime gamer."

"You're better." He grinned. "Now go wipe that smug look off Jae-jin's face."

They both turned, to see the Korean bowing and waving from his side of the stage. Asa, his opponent, was scowling, her arms folded across her white uniform. Clearly, the Norwegian had lost the match.

Which left Spark up against Jae-jin in the final round of solo competition. Winner take all.

Nobody knew which games were going to be selected for the competitions. The early rounds had included puzzles, turn-based battles, and farming sims, as well as a PVP jousting tournament and a crazy spin-race. The space battle had been fun, but Spark wondered what was next.

They wouldn't know until that evening, when the final match began. Rumors flew all over the place, but she tried not to speculate. Not to worry.

All anyone knew for certain was that VirtuMax had created content specifically for the solo category of the World Gaming Championships. Whoever beat it would scoop up their sponsorship—not to mention a fat winner's purse.

Two security guards had been detailed to escort each of the finalists from their rooms to the various tournament events. At first, Spark had thought it was silly—until she saw how the fans pushed forward, begging for autographs, a selfie with her, a lock of her magenta hair.

Without her two guards, she would have been overwhelmed, drowned in a sea of adoration.

Well, mostly adoration.

There were a few griefers with holo-signs saying *Girls Go Home* and *Sidekick Jaxley*. She did her best to ignore them, and to interact with her fans as much as possible without being crushed.

It was exhausting, though, especially as she made her way back to her room to rest up for the final round. She'd never considered this aspect of being a sim-star. Even the national competition hadn't given her this kind of notoriety. If she won, would she be able to handle it?

Jae-jin would, for sure. All the streams and vids showed him acting like the king of the world. Of course, he was mega-famous already, having won the last two years' solo competitions. She'd heard that on the darkweb, he was strongly favored to win. Millions of credits were riding on the outcome of the championship.

And her entire future.

Don't think about that.

Spark stepped through the door of her hotel suite. One of the guards stayed outside, while the other, a woman named Pril, came in with her. The noise lessened as the door slid closed, and Spark let out a sigh of relief.

"You're doing good," Pril said. "Hang in there."

"I thought you didn't game," Spark said with a tired smile.

"Yah, I don't. But my kids do." The guard gave her a serious look. She pretty much always looked serious. "Get some rest, then eat something."

It was good advice. Spark nodded and went to the inner bedroom, leaving the guard behind. A nap was a good idea. She'd pretty much adjusted to the time change, but adrenaline had kept her up the night before, tossing and turning in the unfamiliar bed.

Now though, the cushioned platform looked way inviting. Shower first, though. Her dark green gaming uniform was sticky and probably a little smelly. For the final round, she'd be changing into the fancy turquoise costume sponsored by Zing. They'd coughed up some money, too, though most of her expenses had been covered by that one coin of Papa's she'd sold.

She'd felt so guilty, going through the stack of silver dollars, pricing them on the 'net. But he'd been right. One of them, with a beautiful woman's head on one side, had been worth a lot.

The rest weren't nearly as valuable, and she'd put them back in the beat-up plastic box and tucked it under the mattress. Did her parents even know the collection was there?

Once she got home, she'd "find" them while making the bed or something. But first, she had a championship to win.

～

Spark waited in the wings, trying to calm her jitters. She tucked her hands under her arms to warm up her fingers and concentrated on breathing. Her heartbeat pulsed in her throat, but she knew that once she got in the sim chair, she'd be okay. On the brightly-lit stage, the announcer was thanking the sponsors, especially VirtuMax.

Jae-jin arrived, surrounded by a retinue of women in gauzy dresses and men in suits. He glanced at Spark, lip curling.

"You're going to lose," he said, his tone flat. "Time to go home, gamer-girl."

One of the women giggled, though it wasn't funny.

Spark arched an eyebrow at him—a move that always worked on her brother. "We'll see."

Before he could throw any more insults her way, a loud trumpet blast sounded over the speakers. Their cue to enter.

"And now, our final two competitors in the ultimate match of the night," the announcer said in his overly-cheery voice. "Please welcome Spark Jaxley. And our reigning World Champion in the solo-gamer category, Jae-jin Kim!"

The crowd responded with a cheer loud enough it was like a wind, whipping Spark's hair back. She stepped forward, trying not to squint under the glare of the floodlights, and waved as though she could actually see the faces in the audience.

She went to stand beside her sim rig. Jae-jin took his place opposite, and she was glad she couldn't see him scowling at her.

"The competition tonight, as you'll see, will be a dangerous race through a treacherous dungeon." The announcer swept his arm at the huge screens overhead.

"You'll be able to watch as our heroes challenge themselves against this all-new content, specially created by VirtuMax to push them to their limits. Are you ready?"

The audience screamed *yes* in a dozen different languages.

"Gamers?" The announcer turned his slightly ironic smile toward Spark and Jae-jin.

"Always," the champion said, his voice smug. "I am ready to win."

"You'll have to beat me first." Spark shot him a tight grin.

Ignoring the reactions of the crowd, the announcer gestured at them to gear up. "Talk all you like, but the game will make the final decision. Make ready, competitors. Your challenge awaits."

Spark's focus narrowed to the gleaming sim chairs embossed with the VirtuMax logo, the sheen of light across her gaming helmet, the winking, gemlike LEDs on her gloves. The equip was brand new, though it had been tested thoroughly by an impartial tech team to make sure everything was legit.

Three years ago, one of the sim systems had been tampered with, handicapping the favored player. They'd caught it right before the final competition, and since then, the World Gaming Society had been extra careful.

She slid into the chair, pulled on the gloves, and then settled the helmet on her head.

"Our competitors are ready." The announcer's voice sounded slightly muffled from inside Spark's system.

He'd be muted in-game once play began, though he'd be talking pretty much the whole time to the watching crowd, giving a play-by-play along with his sarcastic opinions. He'd been one of the early streamie stars and had used his fame to form an entertainment empire. Whether he'd rather still be a gamer was a moot point. Everybody aged out, eventually.

"And the countdown begins... NOW," he said.

Spark breathed through the spike of adrenaline pulsing through her. Game time.

The visor projected a mysterious forest across her vision: tall trees dusted with silver and starry white blossoms glowing from the shadowy underbrush. Lush fantasy-land-scape music surrounded her. It was peaceful—but she knew that wasn't going to last.

"Welcome, adventurer," the voice-over narration began. "Today you will enter the Forest of Fey to test yourself against the fearsome creatures who dwell therein. Do you have what it takes to become the Champion of the Realm? Choose your character carefully, for there can be only one winner!"

The forest faded, replaced by a character creation interface.

Spark scanned the options, aware she couldn't linger too long. Whoever beat the forest first, won—but the game had already warned it was crucial to make the right decision.

Her first instinct was to grab an avatar with max damage-doing capabilities. But DPS wasn't everything—those characters were usually pretty vulnerable. She had to balance armor/health points, and the possibility of an off-heal, against lethal output.

Three choices scrolled across her vision. Biting the inside of her cheek, she read the short descriptions under each one.

Spellweaver. Too squishy, from the look of the armor stats. Cloth wasn't good at stopping a deadly blade. And no healing capabilities. Though maybe the game would provide a potion or two, once she started play.

Hunter. Maybe. She hesitated. Better armor, but the melee option was limited to a single small dagger. No good, once her foes got inside her arrow-shooting range.

Mercenary. Okay, that was more like it. A character built to take some smashing, mostly with close fighting capabilities, but the throwing knives were a nice touch. No healing or magical abilities—but the best of the options in her option.

Dimly, like the sound of distant waves, she heard the audience cheering. Had Jae-jin gotten in-game ahead of her?

Pulse racing, she selected the Mercenary. She'd have to learn on the fly.

Her golden-armored character appeared, standing in a small clearing surrounded by dark trees. A fern-edged path led into the shadows.

Quickly, she checked the commands, running through the small hand gestures that controlled her character. Thumb to index finger unsheathed the massive two-handed broadsword strapped on her back and snapped the Mercenary into battle stance. Holding down her middle finger brought up a small target, vision-directed. She looked at the trunk of the nearest tree and flicked her finger up. *Thunk.* One of her throwing knives vibrated from the bark, dead center.

"You have entered the Forest of Fey," the deep-voiced narration said. "Your quest is to reach the center clearing and recover the Queen's Chalice."

A quick cutscene showed a bejeweled silver cup placed on a marble altar. Two monsters guarded it—one a wyvern-like creature with scaly wings and two heads, the other a red-eyed wolf with glowing teeth.

Great. She'd have to defend from simultaneous air and ground attacks. And of course there would be other battles along the way—plus a variety of traps to look out for.

Still, the whole encounter was designed to be over in about thirty minutes. Long enough to run plenty of advertising, without the audience getting too bored and downvoting the contest.

"You have been given a Vial of Restoration and a Vial of Flame to aid you," the voice continued. "Use them well, for once consumed, they are gone forever. And now, adventurer, best be on your way. May the Queen's blessing travel with you."

Her character was momentarily surrounded by a silver glow. A quick stat check showed that she'd been given a stamina buff, upping her health points for thirty minutes. So, her guess about the length of play time was right. She'd better get to the final fight before the buff wore off.

She checked the interface, finding two small icons representing her vials and a small map in the corner of her view. Her character was represented by a glowing orange dot at the southern edge of the forest, and at the center was a cup icon.

A few trails snaked through the woods. The one leading from her clearing went off to the northwest for some distance before intersecting with one headed east. From that path, a spur went straight up to the clearing, while the main trail wound around and entered it from the opposite direction.

Staying on the roads was always the safest choice. But this was also a timed challenge.

The route would be a lot shorter if she cut directly

through the forest, but she'd lose time in fighting the creatures that would doubtless be roaming the woods. Or she could do the expected and stick to the path, trying to make quick work of the traps and mobs lying in wait.

Which way to go?

Another cheer washed against the edges of her concentration. Clearly Jae-jin was already engaging in battle. Surely he couldn't be that far ahead of her—which meant the first encounter wasn't too far up the trail.

Spark strode to the edge of the clearing and glanced down the path. For a moment she wavered—but she hadn't made it this far by playing it safe.

She pointed her character due north, right for the middle of the forest. With a quick prayer for luck, and a tip of her thumb, she strode into the underbrush.

For the first few paces, everything was calm and quiet. Too quiet.

Sunlight flickered through the tall trees, dappling the thick-leaved shrubs with light. The graphics were prime. She hoped the viewers were enjoying the top-quality visuals, because she couldn't afford to get distracted by admiring the immersive detailing on the purple-veined flower petals.

Something rustled overhead.

She dodged to the side, sword raised. An evil-looking troll dropped from above, daggers slicing the air where she'd just been. It landed, red eyes glowing from its dark green face, sharp tusks bared.

"Intruder," it growled. "Die now."

"Not in my plans," she said, going on the offensive.

Her broadsword attack swiped across the troll's chest. It

let out a cry and fell back, but unfortunately the blow wasn't fatal. Black blood trickled sluggishly from the wound.

Without warning, it charged forward. She barely got her sword up in time to block the double-bladed attack. The troll whirled, too fast, and managed to land a stab to her shoulder.

Pain spiked through the sim system, along with a flash of warning yellow around her character, and she winced. Time to end this fight.

She pulled her blade back, then ran it point-first through the troll's midsection. It let out a gargle and slumped over. The enemy health meter in the corner of her vision plummeted into the yellow, then red, then went black.

Dimly, she heard the crowd cheering. She lifted one golden-gauntleted fist in acknowledgement, then sent her character into a run. Every second counted.

Instead of heading in a straight line, she zigzagged through the trees. Her peripheral vision caught a faint greenish glow off to her left, smack in the middle of the direct route up to the Queen's Chalice.

One trap avoided. She hoped.

Before she could get complacent, though, a vine snaked out from the underbrush and twisted around her ankle. She caught her balance and slashed at it, but even as it parted, a second vine fastened around her leg.

"I don't think so," she muttered.

Holding her sword blade parallel to her body, she spun in a circle. Bits of vegetation went flying as more sucker-like vines tried—and failed—to grab her.

She wasn't in-game to prune plants, though, and clearly the point was to immobilize her in place. Which meant she needed to move. Immediately.

Hacking at the last few tendrils, she quickly backed out of range. Only to step on a large white mushroom that had popped up underfoot.

Crap!

Holding her breath, she danced and dodged, trying to get away from the still-seeking vines without stepping on another fungus. The one she'd trodden on was turning bright red and swelling up. An explosion of some kind was coming: sleeping spores, or thorn damage, or a nasty mob spawn.

She had to be gone by the time it exploded, and the only clear path led back the way she'd come. Retreat wasn't an option, though. She had an uneasy feeling that Jae-jin was getting close to the chalice, and she'd learned to trust her gut about gaming. Not to mention that the increased volume outside her sim helmet was a serious sign that things were heating up.

Okay then. Forward, as fast as she could go, and hope this wasn't a Leeroy Jenkins situation.

Making sure her Vial of Restoration was at the ready, she sent her character hurtling forward.

Pop! Pop!

Mushrooms sprouted underfoot. She dashed over them recklessly. Behind her, the first fungus exploded in a shrieking, fleshy shower of red. Oh, not good.

She swung the viewpoint angle around in a one-eighty to see a scarlet demon clamber out of the mushroom carcass. It lifted its scaly hands and out shot a torrent of fire, like a flamethrower targeted on her character.

Ducking, she sent her Mercenary into a forward roll, crushing more fungi along the way.

Good thing she hadn't cued up the Vial of Flame—

chances were these monsters were immune to fire damage. But she had to get out of there, stat.

Despite her dodge, a bit of flame had tagged her and was slowly eating a hole in her armor. Already, her health points were dipping. Damage-over-time spells were the worst, especially if they stacked up. Which she was betting these would.

Another mushroom exploded, and she dashed behind a nearby tree. This time, she avoided the fire blast entirely. If she could keep line-of-sighting the explosions, she just might make it out alive.

A third demon popped up, and this time she wasn't so lucky, catching the edge of the area-of-effect spell. As she'd feared, the slow-burn damage multiplied. Not enough to take her down. Not yet, anyway. Two or three more hits, though...

At least the mushrooms had stopped spawning underfoot.

Boom! Fire engulfed her character. Her armor turned golden-red, and she watched in dismay as her health plummeted to the halfway point. Keeping her fingers mashed together, she sent her character staggering forward.

Tick. Her Mercenary fell to one-quarter health.

Keeping the camera pointed behind her, she managed to yank her character behind a thick shrub as two more flame demons emerged, deadly fire spraying from their fingertips.

Almost out of range.

Almost dead, too.

Just a little farther.

Her finger hovered, ready to pop the Vial of Restoration. Adrenaline shimmered through her, every sense poised.

Not yet.

Not yet.

Red light flashed alarmingly around her character, signaling imminent death.

Now.

She consumed the vial, turning her corpse lurch into a sudden sprint forward as the Mercenary's health regenerated to full.

Spark let out her breath, practically oblivious to the deafening cheers. That had been close. A quick camera pivot showed she was out of range of the deadly demon-spawning mushrooms.

Ahead, the trees thinned, a soft silvery glow filling the air. She slowed her headlong rush, senses on alert. Either another trap awaited or she'd made it to the clearing holding the Queen's Chalice. Or both.

Probably both.

Two-handed sword at the ready, she stepped forward. Silvery mist softened the trees, and a faint chiming music filtered through the air.

She darted a glance at the map readout to make sure she hadn't wandered too far east or west. Nope. According to the mini-map, she'd reached the edge of the clearing where she'd find the Queen's Chalice.

It was hard to see much of anything, though. Was that shape the altar, or one of the creatures guarding it?

A red-eyed wolf leaped at her, answering that question. At least she was in the right place. She swung at the wolf, but it twisted out of range.

Another shape coalesced out of the mist overhead, two-headed and borne on scaly wings, but Spark had been waiting. Narrowing her eyes, she managed to get two daggers off before the wyvern closed with a screech.

Of course the wolf attacked at the same time, but she was ready. Dodging the wyvern's raking claws, she switched targeting to the wolf and triggered her Vial of Flame.

The creature howled as it fur caught fire, but it still leaped for her throat. She swiped at it and it fell back, flames flickering over its body.

The wyvern screeched and plummeted toward her, deadly claws outstretched. Spark pulled back her blade, judging the creature's trajectory. With all her strength, she sliced across its neck. With a satisfying squishy plop, one of the heads landed on the moss-covered ground.

Cheers washed over her, but the fight wasn't done—not by a long shot. The wolf attacked, only slightly slowed by fire damage, and managed to land a bite to her leg. Her Mercenary stumbled, health points dipping.

She danced away, slinging another throwing dagger at the wyvern as it lurched overhead. Both creatures were dying—but too slowly. Time to take one of them out, and hope the other one didn't kill her in the meantime.

Targeting the wolf again, she charged forward. It slid away from her first strike, but she let the momentum of her swing pull her around and managed to injure it on the backstroke.

Yellow light flashed around the Mercenary. The wyvern had struck her head, tearing off her helmet. Oh, that wasn't good.

The wolf growled and leaped. At the last moment, Spark dodged aside and stabbed it through the neck. Weakened by the Vial of Flame, the creature collapsed, its health snuffing out.

One down. One to go.

Spark dropped to her knees, which put her in dagger-throw distance from the wyvern. She only had one blade left. Had to make this one count.

With a steadying breath, she targeted the creature's remaining head, focusing on the eye. It didn't cooperate, thrashing around like, well, like a monster with one head cut off.

Then that moment of perfect clarity, the millisecond pause. She released her last blade.

It struck the wyvern in its shiny yellow eye—a critical blow. Screeching, the creature plummeted to the ground, its health bar black.

She'd done it. But had she beat Jae-jin?

Spark strode up to the white marble altar. The Queen's Chalice stood in the center of the polished surface, gleaming a brilliant silver. She reached to take it—

"Not so fast, would-be Champion," a clear voice rang out. "No one takes my chalice without a fight."

Ah, dammit. She should have known there'd be one final boss.

Spark pivoted, to see an elf woman clad in silver armor that shone as brightly as the chalice. On the queen's head was a tiara of white gems, and she carried two blades—one a wickedly thin rapier, the other a sharp-edged sword.

"You have come this far," the queen said. "A pity you must meet your doom."

She waved one delicate hand, and the health buff Spark had carried since the beginning of the game disappeared. Her health dipped, and she swallowed. All her advantages gone—her throwing daggers, her vials, her extra stamina.

"I don't suppose we can talk this out?" she asked, bringing her sword up.

The elf queen let out a lilting laugh. "I do not bargain with mortals. Besides, you killed my beloved pets."

"You can get new ones." Spark rolled onto the balls of her feet. The queen's attack was imminent—she could feel it.

Before her enemy could spring at her, Spark dove forward. She braced the broadsword's pommel against her chest and threw all her weight behind it, driving it into the queen's chest.

Yellow flashed as the queen's blades struck at the Mercenary's sides, but it was too late for the elf queen. Even as Spark's health dipped, the queen's went faster.

Even dying, she was gracefully beautiful. Her body slumped, silvery-white hair fanning out over the flower-starred moss. A single drop of ruby red blood formed where Spark had struck her.

Not sure why, Spark whirled, grabbed the chalice off the altar, and caught the drop of blood as it fell.

A fanfare of trumpets blasted as the inside of the cup glowed, like she'd caught a supernova in its depths. She blinked, and when her vision cleared she saw the elf queen, now dressed in a gauzy green gown, standing before her.

Two hunky elf dudes flanked the queen, one with yellow eyes, the other with hair the color of a wolf's pelt.

"Oh, well done my brave warrior," the queen said. "Not only have you gained the chalice, you have broken the spell laid upon my consorts. I now declare you the Champion of the Forest of Fey!"

More light and music, and then the scene faded. The game was done.

Spark sat for a moment, heartbeat racing. Sweat itched the back of her neck.

Had she won?

She squashed the impulse to remain inside her helmet. Win or lose, it was over, and she couldn't delay the comfort of not knowing any longer. And no matter what, she'd remember to smile. To be gracious, and not arrogant. Or desolated.

With a deep breath, she pulled off her sim helmet.

Deafening cheers greeted her. Fire kindling in her chest, she glanced up at the huge screens overhead.

WINNER flashed in glowing letters.

Beside Jae-jin's name.

She squeezed her eyes shut for a bare second, just long enough to push back the threat of tears. Long enough to send an apology out into the void.

I'm sorry, Papa.

She'd done her best. But it hadn't been enough.

The rest of the World Gaming Championships were pretty much torture. Her ticket home wasn't for two days, and in the meantime she had to smile and shake hands, congratulate an oh-so-smug Jae-jin, deal with the inevitable griefers gloating over the fact that "girls can't compete at this level."

Most her fans were great, though, and super supportive. They even started a petition to name Spark the winner, since she'd found some bonus end-content—namely, saving the elf queen—that Jae-jin had missed.

The commission was firm, though. Even if they gave

Spark those extra few seconds, the Korean still came out ahead by a slim margin. He'd won the solo championship.

The worst was the VirtuMax ceremony, and seeing her dreams for the future slip away. It was more than winning the money and sponsorship, Spark realized. She'd wanted to be the one representing the company, to prove to kids all over the world that being a kickass gamer wasn't just for boys.

Sure, there were female sim-stars, but the visibility of the VirtuMax spotlight was huge. Especially in places where gamer girls were still fighting to be taken seriously.

At least she wasn't going home empty-handed. The second-place purse was decent. Not mind-bogglingly huge, but enough to help with tuition costs for all three kids in her family. So that was one goal achieved. More or less.

"Good luck next year," her supporters called as she made her farewells. "We know you can do it. Go, Spark!"

Possibly. But without dropping out of school to play all the time, it wasn't going to be easy. And her parents had already made it clear that wasn't an option.

She'd had her shot. And missed.

Her mom picked her up at the airport, and kindly didn't say much. Even Rosie was nice—at least for a few days.

"You could spend the credits yourself," her little sister said as Spark unpacked. "Ooh, I know! Buy a grav-car."

"It's for the family."

"But the family totally could use a new car! Think how prime that'd be." Rosie used her hand to mimic a gliding motion.

Spark shook her head. "Mom and Dad are putting it in a fund for all of us kids to use for university. End of conversation."

Guilt over using Papa's silver dollar to go to Worlds kept her quiet. If only she'd won! Then she'd be able to confess to her family what she'd done. Instead, she was only second-best, and filled with twisty guilt.

With a twinge, she folded away her bright gaming uniforms, sponsors' names emblazoned on the sides. Maybe there'd be another tournament. But probably not.

Three days after she'd gotten home and was resigning herself to her homework, a priority vidcall came through on her tablet.

Spark glanced at the ID and drew in a breath of surprise.

"Who's it from?" Rosie asked, glancing up wide-eyed from her spot on the couch.

"Um." Spark cleared her throat. "VirtuMax."

"Are you sure? It's not a spoof?" Her little sister bounced up and came to hover over Spark's shoulder.

"Looks legit," Spark said. Maybe? Her heart squeezed tight in her chest.

"Then answer it!"

Fingers trembling, Spark slid her vidscreen on. An unsmiling woman stared back at her, the VirtuMax logo prominently displayed on the wall behind her. Spark's heart squeezed tight as she recognized Mrs. Lassiter—CEO of the company.

"Spark Jaxley?" The woman's voice was no-nonsense.

"Yes, that's me."

"Are either of your parents available at this time to take this call with you?"

"My mom is, I think."

Spark shot a look at Rosie, who immediately scooted out of the room to find Mom.

"What's this about?" Spark asked, trying not to hope. "Has something happened to Jae-jin?"

The CEO's expression pinched tight, but she simply shook her head. "As soon as your mother is present, I'll explain."

The next few seconds felt like the longest hours of Spark's life. Finally, her mom came into the living room, drying her hands on a towel. Spark scooted over, making room at the table, and her mother sat.

"I'm Mrs. Jaxley," she said. "Is there a problem?"

The CEO gave them a smile that didn't reach her eyes. "Not necessarily. There is a problem for the champion, however. It's been discovered that Jae-jin accepted cheats and advance information about the challenge from a VirtuMax employee. *Former* employee," she corrected herself.

"Why would Jae-jin do something like that?" Spark blinked. It was crazy to risk his title by cheating—not to mention compromising the whole spirit of the competition. "He could have won on his own."

"It seems he chose to cheat for a very, very large number of credits." The CEO's voice was dry. "I'm sure you're aware there were high stakes bets on the outcome of the World Championships. Some parties wanted to absolutely ensure his victory."

"What does this mean?" Spark's mom leaned forward. "I assume you're calling to do more than just tell us the champion cheated."

"He's not the champion any longer," the CEO said. "Your daughter is."

Spark felt like she was on a simulation flight and the bottom had just dropped out—terrifying and exhilarating all at once. Adrenaline flooded her body as the words penetrated. In the background, she could hear Rosie squealing with delight.

"We'd like to offer her the VirtuMax sponsorship," the CEO continued. "However, since she's a minor, we require parental permission."

"Please, Mom," Spark said, barely breathing.

Her mother firmed her lips and didn't say anything.

"It's a wonderful opportunity," the CEO said. "And of course, we have the best tutors available to make sure Spark's education remains top notch."

"And it pays well," Spark reminded her mom.

"No more potatoes for dinner," Rosie chanted, dancing around the room.

"Sh." Spark sent her sister a narrow-eyed glance. Mom hadn't said *yes* yet.

"I need to discuss this with my husband." Her mom folded her hands in her lap. "He'll be home later this evening."

"I'll give you my private number," the CEO said. "Let me know as soon as you make up your minds. And I urge you not to deprive your daughter of this chance."

Mom only nodded, her expression thoughtful.

"Thank you, Mrs. Lassiter," Spark said. "We'll contact you soon."

"Good." The CEO ended the call and the screen went dark.

Spark stared at her reflection in the black glass. She wanted to beg Mom to say yes, but she knew better. Her parents would discuss it at length, and whatever they chose would be final. It was crucial she show she was mature enough to abide by their decision—and that meant no hysterical pleading.

Even though this was the one thing she wanted most in the world.

"Well?" Rosie demanded, fetching up against the edge of the table and staring at their mom. "You're gonna say yes, right?"

"She has to talk it over with Dad." Spark pulled in a deep breath and turned toward her mother. "Also, Mom, there's something I need to tell you."

Her mother's eyebrows rose, but she didn't say anything. Just waited.

"Before Papa..." Spark cleared her throat. "Before he died, he told me to take his silver dollar collection and sell it in order to get to Worlds. I lied to you when I told you the school had a donor who gave the money for me to go."

Mom nodded slowly, her expression patient. And maybe a little approving?

"Wait." Spark stared at her mom. "You knew?"

"Don't forget." Mom gave her a tiny, sad smile. "Your credit account is linked to ours. We saw the deposit from the auction site, and figured it out."

"And you didn't say anything?" Shame washed hotly across Spark's cheeks.

"Your dad wanted to. But I said wait and see. I argued you were responsible enough to tell us on your own." Mom smiled, and it was beautiful. "Thanks for proving me right."

"Wow." Spark let out a shaky breath. "If I hadn't confessed, would you have let me take the VirtuMax sponsorship?"

Mom shook her head. "But you did. And I think that's proof enough that you're ready—that you can handle the consequences of your actions responsibly and maturely. Even if you're just sixteen."

Spark slumped back in the chair, tears of relief tightening her throat. She'd almost messed up severely. "This was an even harder challenge than winning the World Championship."

"Trust your gut, honey. It always knows what's right." Mom stood up. "Now give me a hug, and go pack."

The press conference lights were blinding, but Spark smiled at where she knew the vidcams were. She couldn't stop smiling, in fact.

Ever since the VirtuMax grav-car had picked her up, she'd been in a whirlwind dream: getting fitted for her new gaming suits, getting set up in a condo of her own, getting her magenta hair brightened...

"It's your signature look, darling," the hair and makeup specialist had said. "We have to emphasize it. And, oh, what it does for your eyes!"

"Miss Jaxley," one of the interviewers said. "We hear that VirtuMax has big plans. Care to elaborate?"

"I can't say much." Spark grinned at the man. "But I can tell you that VirtuMax is working on pushing the limits of sim gaming with their new FullD prototype. From what I've seen so far, it'll be like nothing you've ever experienced."

At least, according to the advance prep she'd had. The system was still a year out from prototype, but viewing the mockups and hearing what the developers had planned, the FullD was going to transform simulation games. If they could pull it off.

Which, judging by the resources VirtuMax was throwing into the project, they would.

And Spark would be there on the forefront, playing the prototype, going all over the world to demonstrate the new system.

Keeping up with her schoolwork, a little voice reminded her.

Okay, yes. But that was only a part of the adventure. The rest was going to be amazing.

She could hardly wait.

ACKNOWLEDGMENTS

Thank you to my team: Laurie Temple, editor extraordinaire, Cover goddess Ravven, Arran McNichol, fabulous copyeditor, and Ginger for the usual great catches.

Resources used include: Katharine M. Briggs, *An encyclopedia of fairies: Hobgoblins, brownies, bogies, and other supernatural creatures* and *Faeries* by Froud, Larkin, and Lee.

OTHER WORKS

THE FEYLAND SERIES

What if a high-tech game was a gateway to the treacherous Realm of Faerie?

THE FIRST ADVENTURE - Book 0 (prequel)

THE DARK REALM – Book 1

THE BRIGHT COURT – Book 2

THE TWILIGHT KINGDOM – Book 3

FAERIE SWAP - Book 3.5

TRINKET (short story)

SPARK - Book 4

BREAS'S TALE - Book 4.5

ROYAL - Book 5

MARNY - Book 6

CHRONICLE WORLDS: FEYLAND

FEYLAND TALES: Volume 1

VICTORIA ETERNAL

Steampunk meets Space Opera in a British Galactic Empire that never was...

PASSAGE OUT

STAR COMPASS

STARS & STEAM

COMETS & CORSETS

THE DARKWOOD CHRONICLES

Deep in the Darkwood, a magical doorway leads to the enchanted and dangerous land of the Dark Elves~

ELFHAME

HAWTHORNE

RAINE

SHORT STORY COLLECTIONS

TALES OF FEYLAND & FAERIE

TALES OF MUSIC & MAGIC

THE FAERIE GIRL & OTHER TALES

THE PERFECT PERFUME & OTHER TALES

COFFEE & CHANGE

MERMAID SONG

ABOUT THE AUTHOR

Growing up, Anthea Sharp spent most of her summers raiding the library shelves and reading, especially fantasy. She now makes her home in the sunny Southern California, where she writes, plays the fiddle, and tries not to game *too* much. Visit her website at antheasharp.com, friend her on Facebook, and be the first to know about new releases and reader perks by subscribing to Anthea's new release newsletter, Sharp Tales, at www.subscribepage.com/AntheaSharp